PLENTY TO (

Plenty, FL 1

Lara Valentine

MENAGE AMOUR

Siren Publishing, Inc.
www.SirenPublishing.com

A SIREN PUBLISHING BOOK
IMPRINT: Ménage Amour

PLENTY TO COME
Copyright © 2012 by Lara Valentine

ISBN: 978-1-62241-178-8

First Printing: July 2012

Cover design by Jinger Heaston
All cover art and logo copyright © 2012 by Siren Publishing, Inc.

Printed in the U.S.A.

PUBLISHER
Siren Publishing, Inc.
www.SirenPublishing.com

DEDICATION

To my handsome husband, who always believed I could write a book, and Jill, the best beta reader I could ask for.

PLENTY TO COME

Plenty, FL 1

LARA VALENTINE
Copyright © 2012

Chapter 1

Cassie Ames smiled as she walked through the tiny but picturesque town of Plenty, Florida. She looked around the serene streets of a town with barely six thousand people and felt at peace. Jillian had been right. It was Jillian Miller, Cassie's best friend, that had come up with the idea of leaving their lives in Chicago far behind and starting over a thousand miles away. They were looking to make a drastic change in their life. Of course, drastic just didn't happen overnight. It had taken a few months for everything to come together.

Jillian had contacted the Teachers for Small Towns nonprofit group and set things in motion. Apparently, small towns had a hard time keeping qualified teachers. With Cassie's minor in mathematics and Jillian's degree in history, they were surprised to find out they were not only qualified to teach school but highly recruited by several small towns. They had chosen this one, sight unseen, on the basis of its proximity to Orlando and Tampa and the warm, inviting letter they had received from the town council.

They had been in Plenty less than a week but were enchanted with their new home. Stepping into downtown Plenty was a little like stepping back in time. The two-lane Main Street ran through the center of town with a speed limit of twenty-five miles per hour. The downtown boasted neat, well-kept stores with friendly merchants. The old-fashioned diner had outdoor seating allowing customers a front row seat of small town life.

The town sprawled out with the park at one end and the historic district at the other. On the corner of Main Street, near the park, was the sheriff's office. Across the street was the hair salon, the grocery store, and the hardware store.

Palm trees lined the streets, along with brightly colored benches for weary shoppers and discreetly placed trash cans and recycling containers. There were no excuses for not recycling.

There was no excuse for not being friendly either. Cassie was used to the big city where eye contact was rare and actual conversation with a stranger unheard of, unless that stranger was yelling in traffic and flipping the bird. Here, people waved, smiled, and stopped to chat. It would take some getting used to, but she already loved the slower pace and the friendly people of Plenty. She should have made this drastic change a hell of a lot sooner.

"So, this pizza place must be just down the street." Jillian's voice brought Cassie out of her daydream. She peered at the signs along one side and then the other side of the street. It couldn't be too far. The downtown just wasn't that big. "There it is! I'm starving!" Jillian exclaimed and began dragging Cassie across the street.

Cassie chuckled and followed her enthusiastic, best friend through the front door of the town's one and only pizza parlor. They both stopped inside the front door and looked around for an empty table. The place was packed and a little noisy. There was a jukebox in the corner playing the latest country tune and waitresses bustling about. It was then that Cassie realized that most of the people in the place were staring, at them.

"Y'all must be the new teachers in town."

Cassie turned toward the friendly voice with quite the twang and found herself looking up. Way up. Cassie knew she was tiny. Heck, she looked up to pretty much everyone, but this was one tall woman.

Gorgeous, too. Cassie was speechless staring at this woman who could have been a model, and apparently Jillian was, too, as she was uncharacteristically silent.

"Y'all just follow me, and we'll get you a table."

Cassie cast a glance at Jillian, who shrugged. So they followed the hostess to a back table away from the jukebox with what felt like every set of eyes in the place following them.

Jillian, as usual, found her voice first. "How did you know who we were?"

"Honey, this is one small town, and not much goes on that everyone doesn't know about. Everyone's talking about the two pretty school teachers that moved into the condos on the edge of town. My name is Charlie, by the way. Short for Charlotte, but I've never been short in my life." Charlie smiled, and Cassie couldn't help but like the woman. She seemed so open and friendly and so different from the tense, almost hostile people she was used to meeting in Chicago. She handed them two menus and continued talking in her soft drawl. "Don't let all these people starin' at you make you uncomfortable. They'll get back to their own business pretty quick. It's just, everyone wants to see the new town residents, that's all. What can I bring you to drink?"

Cassie and Jillian had developed a taste for sweet iced tea in a very short time, and they each ordered one. Charlie turned to get them with a glance and a wink at all the people still looking at them. Cassie could see they were trying to be sly about checking them out, but she almost laughed out loud at how terrible they were at being sneaky.

Jillian, an exuberant redhead with sparkling, green eyes and dimpled smile, was not nearly as reserved as Cassie and simply turned toward the room, gave a huge smile, and waved at them all. Grins and laughs from the patrons followed. Cassie relaxed and also smiled at them. These were her new neighbors, and she wanted to be as friendly as possible.

As she chatted away to Jillian excitedly about the upcoming first day of school, Cassie felt someone staring. She could literally feel a set of eyes that seemed to pull her attention. This wasn't the casual, friendly eyes they had felt earlier but something different, more intense. She turned toward the entrance and stared into the most handsome face she had ever seen. Her eyes went wide as she took in the man whose stare seemed to bore a hole in her.

He was tall, very tall. He had to be six-two or six-three, at least, with broad shoulders that tapered down to a slim waist and powerful legs. His hair was a dark brown, almost black, which made his topaz-blue eyes all the more startling. His face was masculine, with a square jaw and a nose that looked like it had been broken once. He wasn't quite handsome in a classic sense, but he screamed "man" in a way that made her stomach flutter and her heart pound.

Geez, they grow them big and fine looking in this town. This is a man's man.

Her palms started to sweat, and the man gave her a slow smile. The smile reached all the way to his blue eyes and seemed to soften them a little. He had dimples on each side of his mouth, and Cassie fought down the urge to kiss each one of them and run her tongue in the grooves. What was she thinking? She had never had a reaction to a man like this, and honestly, it was really the last thing she needed. A man would just be a complication, and she had enough complications in Chicago to last a lifetime. Two lifetimes, really.

She closed her eyes briefly to get control of herself, and when she opened them, he was still looking at her and obviously amused. Could he possibly have realized the effect he was having on her? She shifted under his gaze, and it was then she realized her panties had gone quite damp, and she was pressing her thighs together to control the moisture starting to pool there.

Get a hold of yourself, girl! He probably has a wife, six kids, a mortgage, and a minivan.

She forced herself to turn back to Jillian, who was looking at her strangely. It was clear Jillian had noticed her reaction to the man, and

Cassie knew she was going to hear about this from her friend. Jillian was always trying to get her to go out, but after Danny Trent in Chicago, Cassie wasn't looking for a man. Especially, a man that looked as good as this gorgeous guy did.

* * * *

"Here's your pizza, Zach. One extra-large with everything." Charlie handed him the steaming-hot pizza box and gave him a big smile. "I see you're hungry for more than pizza, though. She sure is cute. I bet Chase would think so, too." Charlie gave him a knowing look.

Zach Harper had known Charlie for years and had a great affection for her and her three husbands. Charlie had come to town years ago for a photo shoot and stayed after the three Johnson brothers swept her off her feet. She had given up a budding modeling career to open this restaurant with her men and raise a couple of great kids.

"Okay, you caught me looking. She is cute. I guess she's one of the new teachers in town. Sure doesn't look like any of my teachers when I went to school," Zach said, trying to sound a hell of a lot more casual and nonchalant than he actually felt.

Zach couldn't help but sneak another look at the tiny blonde, and his heart seemed to pound a little harder and faster. She was way more than cute, but Zach wasn't in the mood for girly confidences with Charlie. He wanted to stand there all night and stare at the new teacher.

The blonde was absolutely breathtaking, and Zach wasn't able to help himself. She was a tiny thing with long hair and elfin features. Slim, but she still managed to have curves. Curves which looked spectacular in the simple, red sundress she wore. He chuckled to himself a little as he realized he was staring and obviously made her a little uncomfortable. A beautiful woman like her from the city probably got attention from men all the time, but unlike some women he had met, she didn't seem to demand it. She had his attention, all of his attention, including his dick's. His cock had given the blonde the approval right away, swelling against the zipper on his jeans.

Zach shifted a little, trying to ease the pressure and distract his libido from the prettiest girl who had come to Plenty in probably decades. He wondered how he could introduce himself without looking like a complete ass. She would probably notice the tent he was making in his jeans, and he wasn't sure his vocal chords were functioning properly anyway.

Hell, he needed to get out of there before he did something embarrassing. Like walk over to her and beg her to let him kiss her. And it sure wouldn't stop at kissing if his cock was in charge. He would have her bent over the table, taking her from behind, grabbing a handful of her long blonde hair as he drove each of them to their release.

Since he was on the town council and a descendent of one of the town's founding families, doing any of that was not an option. Okay, it wasn't an option at all, no matter who his parents were. She would think he was a lunatic. He took one last look at her, sighed, and turned to walk out the door. A swift glance at Charlie showed her practically doubled over with laughter. He wasn't fooling anyone, least of all himself.

* * * *

"Well, what did you think of the pizza, girls?" Charlie asked as she delivered their check and cleared the table.

"That pizza was heaven," Jillian said, closing her eyes in delight. "Pure heaven. Of course, Cassie ate most of it, as usual."

"I have a fast metabolism," Cassie retorted, used to her friend's teasing about the amount of food Cassie could eat. She could really pack it away, and sometimes it was a trifle embarrassing.

"By the way," Jillian said, "you introduced yourself, but we didn't introduce ourselves. I'm Jillian Miller and this is Cassie Ames, your new customers for life."

"Nice to meet both of you, and welcome to Plenty. My, my, Cassie Ames, you sure got the attention of Zachary Harper. I thought his eyes were going to fall out of his head, he was staring at you so hard. Don't know what spell you cast on him, but that is one smitten man," Charlie said with a grin.

"Ummm…which one was he?" Cassie asked nervously, her eyes looking everywhere but at Charlie.

"You know perfectly well which one he was, missy. Tall, dark, handsome guy staring at you. I saw you lookin' too. No sense denying it. Don't worry. He's one of the good ones. He and his brother, Chase. They belong to one of the founding families here in Plenty. Members of the town council, business owners, run a ranch, real pillar-of-the-community stuff. No woman could do much better than snagging those two. The woman that ends up with those two will be a lucky one. Of course, not as lucky as me. For the last twenty-five years, my husbands have made me the luckiest woman in Plenty. Yes, sir. Nothing like real love." Charlie glanced back at the kitchen and counter where Cassie could see three very handsome men working. But, what did she say?

Jillian, always the less reticent one, asked, "Charlie, what do you mean by husbands? You made it sound plural."

Charlie smiled and shook her head, tsking a little. "I guess they didn't tell you when you took the job, huh?"

"Tell us what?" Cassie asked carefully, a little afraid of the answer.

"Let me put these dishes in the kitchen, and I'll explain everything to you."

As Charlie turned back to the kitchen, Jillian and Cassie shared a look that clearly said, one to the other, "What the hell?"

* * * *

"So, let me get this right. This town has polygamy?" Cassie thought she was going to be dizzy. She had seen a documentary about polygamy. What had she and Jillian gotten into?

"It's not polygamy. It's polyamory or ménageamous. And the men don't take multiple wives. Only the women take multiple husbands. It started back a couple of hundred years ago. Florida was a dangerous, untamed place and it was to a woman's advantage to have more than one husband to take care of her and the children. If something happened to one husband, well, she had a spare. Not to mention, unsettled territory like this didn't have that many women to begin with, so men began sharing a wife. The tradition lives on in Plenty. Of course, not everyone has a plural marriage. Some have a regular monogamous marriage. But folks here are open-minded about things and people. We like it that way," Charlie said. "We want people to live life on their own terms. The only thing different about a ménage marriage is the love. There is more of it."

Cassie calmed down at Charlie's explanation. However, she knew that she could never handle multiple men. One man was trouble enough. She, of all people, should know.

"Well, your husbands are very handsome, and you look very happy," Jillian said with a smile.

"I am. As hard as having three men is, it is worth it. One of them always makes sure that I have someone to talk to, share with, and help with the kids. And I don't mind telling you, the lovin' is really something even after all these years." Charlie grinned, fanning her face with a towel, and Cassie couldn't help but grin back. Charlie really did seem happy, and if no one was getting hurt then this ménageamous thing was fine with Cassie. It was difficult to be against love, after all.

"Of course, you'll find out yourself, Cassie, what loving more than one man is like," Charlie said with a twinkle in her eye.

"What do you mean? I don't have one man, let alone two!" Cassie exclaimed.

"Zachary Harper has a younger brother by a year, Chase Harper, and they share. And the way Zach was looking at you, I am guessing that you'll be meeting him pretty quickly. And Chase is every bit as good looking and hunky as his brother."

Cassie pressed her hands to her hot cheeks at the thought of Zach Harper and the way he had made her feel just by looking at her.

And oh my god, there are two of them? I'll never survive it. Nope, I just need to stay away from Zachary and Chase Harper.

Chapter 2

Cassie strolled alongside Jillian toward the town park where the Labor Day picnic was being held. Their condo was just a few blocks away, so they had decided it would be easier to walk. As they entered the park to look for a picnic spot, she could see that the park was already very full. Good thing they had come early. It looked like there were still a few shady spots to be had.

"How about under that tree, Cass?"

Cassie agreed, and they arranged their blanket and chairs to get a good view of the park and the festivities. One of Cassie's favorite pastimes was "people watching," and it looked like it would be a good day for that.

Cassie stretched out her legs on the picnic blanket and stared up at the blue Florida sky. Not a cloud in sight, and it was hot, way hot. She could feel her bra and panties starting to cling to her damp skin. Labor Day weekend was supposed to signal the end of summer, but summer in Florida didn't retreat, gracefully, until October she had been told. The town park was full of people celebrating with softball, Frisbee, and picnic food, despite the oppressive heat and humidity. Cassie wondered if she would ever get used to the Florida weather.

The last few weeks had been busy, and Cassie had barely had time to contemplate her new life. She and Jillian had been quite busy getting their classrooms together, completing the new teacher orientation, and finalizing their curriculum. The first week of school had been exhausting, but Cassie found she enjoyed teaching. Most of her students were middle school age and were starting to be more interested in the opposite sex than in school, but they were surprisingly well behaved. She had a few troublemakers, but with some good advice from the seasoned teachers, she had learned quickly how to handle them. In fact, several of her students had stopped and talked to her as she and Jillian had set up their picnic blanket. She had met so many parents today, she was sure she would never remember them all, but she vowed to try.

Her eyes scanned the large crowd that had gathered in the park. It seemed like everyone must have turned out and was busy celebrating. Each family was to bring a covered dish, and the town provided the hamburgers, hot dogs, and chicken. Jillian had made her famous pistachio salad, and Cassie had made a batch of blonde brownies. Cassie had found the costs of the picnic were covered by donations from the residents, so she made sure that she and Jillian were generous in that respect. They both wanted their new hometown to know how much they appreciated the warm welcome.

Cassie's eyes landed on a tall, well-muscled man in uniform headed their way. Light-brown hair with blond streaks and a tanned face made him look a little like a Viking, Cassie mused. That Viking body didn't hurt either. Just a few weeks in this town and both she and Jillian had noticed that it had more than its share of drool-worthy men.

Maybe gym membership was mandatory for the men in this town, Cassie thought with a giggle.

That would explain the hard bodies she had seen. The man in uniform stopped right in front of them and gave a smile that would send most women swooning. In fact, Cassie could have sworn she heard Jillian's sharply in-drawn breath.

"Ladies, I wanted to stop by and introduce myself and welcome you to our town. My name is Ryan Parks. I'm the sheriff in this town." He knelt down so that his eyes were even with theirs and seemed to wait for a reply.

For once, Jillian wasn't the first to speak. In fact, she seemed struck dumb, so Cassie quickly tried to smooth over the silence.

"Thank you, Sheriff. Everyone has made us feel real welcome. We already love Plenty."

"That's great to hear," said the sheriff as his eyes strayed to look at Jillian. Cassie noticed her best friend's face was tinged with a little red, and she didn't think it was from the heat. "We take great pride in our little town being a safe, friendly place to live. If either of you girls has any trouble, please let me know."

"Thank you again, Sheriff. This town looks pretty trouble free so far."

"Well, you girls enjoy the picnic." And with that, the sheriff took one last look at Jillian and made his way toward the grandstand.

Cassie eyed her best friend speculatively. Jillian seemed to be having trouble catching her breath, and her cheeks were still quite red. Cassie opened her mouth to ask Jillian what was going on and why she didn't say a word to the sheriff, but Jillian cut her off with a dark look and, "Not a fucking word, Cassie. Not a word."

* * * *

"C'mon, Jillian! Let's go get some food. I'm starved!"

"You're always starved, Cass. I really don't know where you put it all. But I just put sunscreen on, and I want to get a few rays first. Go ahead, and get food if you want."

Cassie started to get up from the blanket when she felt a pair of large, warm hands helping her. She looked up slowly into those topaz-blue eyes that had made such an impression the night at the pizza parlor. Up close, he was even taller than he had looked at the restaurant. He was probably a foot taller than she, and his shoulders were so wide, he seemed to block out the rest of the revelry in the park around her.

"Uhhh…thank you," Cassie managed to stammer.

Mr. Perfect, as she had dubbed him that night at the restaurant, smiled that smile that showed his dimples and warmed his eyes. Man, he was one fine-looking specimen. Her body was reacting to his nearness, and she tried to take a step back, but he just moved closer as he kept hold of her hand. She stared down at it and then at him again, hoping he would get the hint, but he just smiled a little wider and slid his thumb back and forth over her wrist.

Cassie's heart went into overdrive, and she could feel the blood rising in her cheeks and somewhere a little farther south, too. What was it about this man that sent her libido rocketing? He was tall and gorgeous and smelled a little like spice, citrus, and musky male. She felt her nipples pebble and hoped he didn't notice her body's reaction.

"I wanted to introduce myself to our newest town residents. I'm Zachary Harper. My family owns a horse farm outside of town, and we also have a construction business. I hope you're getting settled in and enjoying your new home." His hand continued to hold hers as he said it, and even though he said it to both of them, she felt his gaze on her acutely.

Apparently Jillian had recovered from her encounter with the sheriff since she was the first to speak this time.

"Zachary Harper? Wasn't your name on the letter we got from the town council extolling the virtues of moving to Plenty?"

"Guilty as charged, I'm afraid. Both my brother and I are members of the town council...and lifelong residents." Zach gave Jillian a warm smile but turned back to Cassie as if drawn there.

"Brother? Is he here too?" Jillian gave Cassie a meaningful look that said she remembered the conversation with Charlie that night at the pizza parlor.

"Yes, he wanted to introduce himself, also. Oh, there he is now." Zachary finally turned away from Cassie, and she couldn't help following his gaze and almost fainted. He most definitely had a brother and, damn, if he wasn't as fine and hunky as Charlie had said that night.

Cassie knew her mouth was hanging open a little, but who could blame her? His brother was just as tall, but with slightly lighter brown hair and the most striking, emerald-green eyes she had ever seen. They were fringed with thick, dark lashes that women, including Cassie herself, would kill for. His shoulders were just as broad, and his abs appeared to be just as tight. His face was a little more classically handsome than Zach's with full, sensual lips and a square jaw. Cassie's knees had turned to marshmallows just looking at these two men, and if Zach hadn't still been holding her hand, she probably would have collapsed in a heap of aroused femininity.

Jillian just smiled and shook her head at Cassie's dumbfounded expression. Luckily, Jillian always seemed to come to Cassie's rescue at just the right time, and she wouldn't let her down this time either.

"Well, I'm Jillian Miller and this is my best friend, Cassie Ames. It's very nice to meet you." Jillian extended her hand, and Zach's brother shook it briefly and then lifted Cassie's free hand and just seemed to hold it as his brother did.

"My name is Chase Harper. It's a pleasure to meet both of you."

The men had managed to wedge her between their hard, male bodies, and her libido had woken up and taken notice after months and months of dormancy. Her pussy was creaming at the mere sight and smell of these two men. What would she do if they actually kissed her, for God's sake? She needed to get some space, and soon.

"Actually, I was just headed to the buffet line to get some food," Cassie said a little too quickly. She tried to breathe in some fresh air, but the only thing she inhaled was more of their scent, and another gush of moisture made itself known between her legs. Jillian gave her an odd look, but Cassie just tightened her lips and tried to look over the men's shoulders, but it was mighty hard as they seemed to take up the entire landscape. With her petite height, they blotted out almost her entire view of the park. Their size made her feel very small and feminine.

"Great idea. We would be happy to escort you ladies," Chase said in that silky voice that Cassie knew probably had girls dropping their panties right and left.

"Yes, we can give you some pointers about the local fare," Zach said with a smile that showed those gorgeous dimples and took Cassie's hand and started to lead her toward the food line. Okay, maybe those dimples were what got women wet.

Either way, she didn't think these guys had too much trouble with the opposite sex. And she had had nothing but trouble with the opposite sex, and she needed to remember that, no matter how wet her panties got. They were temptation personified, but it looked like she was trapped into following temptation all the way to the buffet line.

Cassie sighed and let the two gorgeous men lead her away. Or was it astray?

* * * *

Cassie sat on the picnic blanket between two very handsome and attentive men. They had insisted on escorting her to the buffet line. There they had pointed out all the yummy local foods she should try and the food that she should avoid at all costs—just what were tofu salmon cakes anyway? The three of them had settled back down on the blanket with their overflowing plates. Jillian saw some friends and was now on the other side of the park eating with some of the other teachers from the school, leaving Cassie to entertain Zach and Chase all by herself.

She was a little overwhelmed at the attention from such handsome men, but they seemed very nice and down-to-earth as they chatted. They sat close and seemed to take up all the space around her, and they didn't mind invading her personal space at all. In fact, every time she scooted back to get a little breather, they would scoot a little closer. Cassie was now at the back edge of the blanket and there was nowhere else to scoot to. *Fuck.* She had literally backed herself into a corner. All the while, she gave herself a stern talking-to. She didn't need any man troubles. She had enough going on in her life.

Her body didn't seem to want to listen to her brain around those two. Her nipples had long since pebbled and were pushing against her bra which was damp from the sweltering heat. Her panties were soaked and uncomfortable, and her lungs filled with their heady, masculine scent. Her pulse pounded as they talked to her in voices that could only be described as low and sexy. With Zach and Chase around, she simply had trouble catching her breath.

"Ready for dessert?" Chase's smooth voice brought Cassie out of her reverie.

"Yeah, you got to try dessert. Mrs. Carter makes a blackberry cobbler that is practically famous." Zach grinned.

"I am all for dessert, all the time," Cassie said with a smile. "I'll just go get—"

"No, ma'am," Chase interjected. "I will be most happy to get you a plate of dessert. I'll get you a little bit of everything and then, when you find your favorite, we can get you a big plate of it."

"You don't have to do that. I can get my own food." Cassie tried to protest but could see the set of their jaws. She wasn't going to win this one.

"Sit back, and let us spoil you a little." Zach leaned forward and tucked a flyaway hair behind her ear. His breath was warm on her cheek. His fingers lingered for longer than they needed and slid slowly down her cheek, her throat, shoulder, arm, and then finally her hand where he laced his fingers through hers. His hand felt big and warm and—safe. Yes, safe. Cassie hadn't felt safe, really safe, in a very long time. It seemed the last eighteen months had been filled with nothing but obsession and evil. She couldn't help but be a little relieved that she could still recognize goodness and safety when she saw it. And these men were good, she knew that. She could tell that they would take good care of her. They just needed to understand that they didn't have to. She could take care of herself. She always had before.

"Okay, but nothing with nuts. I'm allergic to nuts, and I love chocolate."

"Yes, ma'am. No nuts and plenty of chocolate. Be right back. While I'm gone, Zach, ask Cassie about Friday night."

Cassie turned to Zach. "What about Friday night?"

Zach smiled warmly at Cassie. Her heart skipped a few beats. "We want to take you to the drive-in on Friday night. It's a lot of fun. Our parents used to take us there when we were kids. We would wear our pajamas and fall asleep in the back seat with a pile of pillows and blankets. Friday is a double creature feature. Please say you'll come."

"Creature feature?" Cassie couldn't help but laugh. These men were surprising.

"Yep, the owner of the drive-in loves horror movies. New ones, old ones, good ones, bad ones. He doesn't care, he just likes them. And, well, Chase and I like horror movies, too. Besides, there is nothing like a scary movie to get a pretty girl to cuddle up close." Zach gave her that grin that showed off his dimples. There really ought to be a law against a man looking that good.

"Well, you have discovered my shameful secret. I love horror movies, too. And this girl won't be cowering at buckets of blood, no, sir. I say bring it on."

"Then bring it on we shall."

Chase plopped down next to them with a plate overflowing with sweets. "Is she coming Friday night?"

"It turns out she is hiding a bloodlust. She's coming all right and says she's not going to be cowering next to us. Nope, she doesn't get scared."

Chase gave a hearty laugh, and his eyes twinkled. "We'll see about that. Some of those movies can be pretty scary, you know."

"Nothing scares me," Cassie said before biting into a slice of chocolate cake. She closed her eyes in ecstasy. *Hell yeah, chocolate, baby.*

"Looks like we found another of your weaknesses," Zach said with a grin as he watched her wolf down the plate of sweets.

"Yes, I really love chocolate...and well, sweets in general. I'm lucky to have a fast metabolism. But I try to stay in shape, too. I like to run, mainly."

"Chase runs, too. I prefer biking myself." Zach stretched his muscled legs out on the blanket, and Cassie couldn't help but notice how great they looked. They were firm and tan.

"I like to bike, too, but there weren't many places to bike safely in Chicago. Maybe I'll have to get a new bike since there are so many great places to go around here."

Cassie started to relax as she chatted with the men about her life in Chicago and how much she liked Plenty. They were very easy to talk to and seemed interested in just about everything she had to say. They made it hard to resist them when they behaved that way. Of the two of them, Cassie noticed that Chase did most of the talking. He was funny, and he liked to tease quite a bit. He had an easygoing air about him that was nice to be around after all the drama in her life. She could imagine talking to him for hours. He never seemed to run out of conversation.

Zach, on the other hand, was much quieter. He rarely broke into the conversation unless he really had something to say. He paid attention to what she was saying with an intensity she had never experienced before. While Chase radiated playfulness and charm, Zach radiated authority and power. Chase would probably charm the panties off women, and Zach would simply hold out his hand and calmly ask for them. She was sure women rarely refused either of them.

They talked a little about their life, too, and she found out that not only did they help run their family horse farm but also owned their own construction company.

"Wow, you guys must be very busy to do all that!" Cassie said with a grin.

"We like to keep busy, and with two other brothers to help run the farm when they aren't in school, it isn't that bad. Now that the construction company is a success, we work a little less than we used to. When it was really struggling, it seems like we were working twenty-four hours a day and then some."

Zach nodded in agreement as his brother spoke.

"In fact," said Zach, "we built the condos where you live. We finished them recently and are very proud of the project. I hope everything is okay there. If you have any problems, be sure to let us know, and we will come out and fix it right away. We have a crew that just does home repair."

"You built the condos? They're great. No issues whatsoever. In fact, Jillian and I were saying that it's the nicest place we have ever lived. Most of the buildings in Chicago are older, and they always seem to have a lot of issues that need to be repaired."

As the day turned into evening, Cassie talked to Zach and Chase about just about everything and found that she really liked them. She liked the fact that person after person stopped and talked to them through the afternoon. It seemed everyone knew them, and everyone liked them. Many people asked them their opinion about civic affairs, horses, or construction, and she was impressed they were so well-respected. Her natural reticence melted away, and she found herself wishing the day didn't have to end.

Jillian came back for the evening fireworks, and afterward Zach and Chase insisted on walking both of them home.

"Really, Jillian and I will be fine," Cassie protested. "We're just a few blocks down the street."

"Yeah, we know, Cassie. We built the condos, remember?" Chase said with a teasing smile.

Cassie blushed a little at his tone.

"Relax, it's no trouble at all. Our mama would be scandalized if we didn't walk you home. This is Plenty, not Chicago, and this is how a gentleman treats a lady."

Cassie opened her mouth to protest again, and then quickly shut it. He was right. This was how a gentleman should treat a lady. She just had never met anyone who knew that.

"Thank you, then. We would be grateful for the escort."

Chapter 3

The week passed quickly for Cassie, and she and Jillian headed for the hair salon after school on Friday. Cassie wanted to get her hair trimmed before her date, and Jillian decided that she could use a trim, too. They walked into the hair salon, the Snip and Sing, and Cassie took in the ultramodern design. The counter tops and sinks were all stainless steel and seemed to gleam. The floor appeared to be a shiny stone of some kind that swirled different shades of blue. The chairs were black leather and the walls painted a muted blue-gray. As she scanned the room, her gaze went to the back of the salon where several couches were placed before what appeared to be a small stage. And that's when Cassie's eyes flew open with surprise.

Two older women, both in plastic capes to protect their clothes and with foils in their hair, were standing on that small stage in the back of the salon…singing. Singing the Dixie Chicks, to be exact, and Cassie couldn't help but gape at the sight before her. It was so bizarre that it took a few moments to realize that the women singing were really awful but more than made up for that with their enthusiasm. They seemed to be having the time of their lives, in fact, if their smiles were any indication.

"Hey, ladies. You must be Cassie and Jillian."

Cassie and Jillian turned and saw the smiling face of a pretty blonde about their age.

"I'm Rebecca and will be doing your hair today." She grinned at them and gave them a look that said they could go ahead and ask.

Jillian spoke first, as usual. "Okay, I'll ask. What's up with the karaoke?"

Rebecca started laughing, and Cassie and Jillian joined in although not sure what they were laughing at except the strangeness of the situation.

"Let's get you shampooed, and I'll explain while I cut your hair."

An assistant washed their hair and led them to Rebecca's booth, which was at the front of the salon overlooking the bustling Main Street. As Rebecca started on Jillian's hair first, she explained, trying to keep a straight face but failing miserably.

"When I graduated from hair dressing school, my father said he would open up my own hair salon for me. I'd own it, but I had to let him have karaoke in the back. He loves karaoke, and the bar down the street had discontinued their Friday night sings. By the way, in addition to being your hairdresser and DJ today, I am also your neighbor. I live two doors down from you in the condo complex."

Cassie had to smile at how everyone in a small town was connected in some way. This was one of the things she loved about living there.

As Rebecca worked on Jillian's hair, they chatted and made plans for a "girl's night in" the next night—pizza and a chick flick.

Rebecca laughed. "You'll get used to how quiet a small town is. Our girl's night in is about the most exciting thing I have done in weeks."

At that moment, a tall, broad-shouldered, older, but still quite handsome man walked into the hair salon carrying a large box.

"Hi, baby! I picked up that box for your brother from the hardware store. Has he been by yet, and has Steve called?" he asked.

"Not yet, Dad. Let me introduce you to the newest town residents. Cassie Ames, Jillian Miller, this is my dad, Mike Parks, or better known around here as DJ Mike."

The older man roared with laughter at that remark and only stopped when another man walked into the salon.

"Oh, Steve, I thought you were going to call when you got done with your last patient." Mike Parks wrapped his arms around the other very handsome man and gave him a loving kiss.

"Get a room, you two!" Rebecca laughed, but didn't seem too upset at the public display of affection from her father. In fact, she looked downright indulgent.

Cassie had to smile herself. It was obvious the two men were very in love. In fact, this was what she loved so much about Plenty. They were tolerant and open. They embraced everyone and didn't care about social constraints. She loved this nonjudgmental town.

Steve and Mike hurried to the back of the salon, grabbed a cola, and began to blow off steam singing—in excellent voices—a rock song from the seventies. The two women in foils from earlier were now finished but were apparently hanging around to join Mike and Steve as backup singers.

"Great way to end the week, huh?" Rebecca laughed. "Those guys are two peas in a pod. They'll be back there rockin' out until I close tonight. They are really in love, too. I hope I find love like that someday." Rebecca sighed.

Cassie couldn't help but ask, "How did your dad and Steve get together?"

Becca's eyes got a little sad. "My mom was in a terrible car accident. A drunk driver crossed the yellow line and hit her head on. Steve was the doctor on duty. He had the unenviable task of telling us that Mom was gone. He was so sweet and caring to all of us. His wife had also passed a few years before from breast cancer. Months later, Steve and Dad got a cup of coffee, and well, they fell in love. No one was more surprised than they were, although, our whole family was pretty shocked. But they're happy, and I want my dad to be happy. Steve's a great guy, too, and a terrific doctor."

Before Cassie could reply, the door opened, and the sheriff strode in. He really was a handsome man, and Cassie sneaked a look at Jillian, who appeared to be a little stunned by his presence.

"Oh hey, Ryan! Dad brought your stuff from the hardware store. The box is in the back room. Have you met Cassie and Jillian?"

"Thanks, Becca, and yes, I had the pleasure of meeting them at the picnic. How are you, ladies?" He smiled warmly at them both but seemed to look more directly at Jillian.

Cassie looked sideways at Jillian, who seemed unable to speak at the moment.

"We're fine, Sheriff, thank you for asking. We didn't realize that Rebecca was your sister."

"Yep, got a brother, too. Jackson is a firefighter and two years younger than me. Rebecca is the baby and two years younger than Jack." The sheriff looked at Jillian, although, it had been Cassie who had spoken. He moved a little closer to Jillian and spoke to her directly this time. "And how are you today, Miss Jillian?" His voice was so smooth and warm, and Jillian looked positively panicked at his proximity.

But Jillian was not one to be panicked for long. With as much dignity as a woman could muster wearing a plastic cape and Velcro rollers, Jillian answered the sheriff, "Fine, thank you, Sheriff. And yourself?"

"Much better for seeing you today, Miss Jillian." The sheriff smiled a devastating smile and walked to the back of the salon to speak to his father.

Rebecca smiled at Jillian as she glanced at her brother. "Ryan really is the nicest guy. He and Jackson are looking for a nice girl, and I think Ryan really likes you, Jillian. But he is a little shy when it comes to women. Jackson is the more outgoing one."

"They share, too?" Cassie wondered just how many men in the town did that.

"Yep, they like to share. We didn't grow up in a ménageamous home, but they still want to be like many of their friends. Now Zach and Chase, they grew up in a home with two fathers, so it probably seems very natural to them."

Cassie looked surprised when Rebecca mentioned Zach and Chase, but Rebecca just laughed.

"Honey, there are no secrets in a town this small. Everyone knows that Zach and Chase got their eye on you. Other than my own brothers, those guys are two of the best you will ever find. Hard working and honest as the day is long. You'll do fine with them. They deserve the best. A hell of a lot better than what they had. That bitch Amelia did nothing but use them and make them miserable. She treated them like trained poodles. Good riddance to her!"

This was a new name to Cassie, and although she wanted to respect the men's privacy, she had to ask, "Amelia? I haven't heard of her."

"No, you probably wouldn't have. Amelia grew up here in Plenty. She was the only child of one of the founding families, and spoiled is not too strong a word. Her daddy gave her everything she wanted and then some. She also wanted Zach and Chase, and for a while everything was okay, I guess. She treated them horribly in my opinion. She expected them to spoil her the way her daddy always had. She treated them like hired help and demanded they buy her things. They were just getting their construction business going at the time. They must have been working around the clock, but all Amelia did was piss and moan at them about every little thing. Eventually, she took a trip to Dallas to visit a friend and came back with a rich attorney fiancé. Married him a few months later and lives in Dallas now. As I said before, good riddance to trash. I know you'll treat them with more kindness than she ever did."

Cassie was appalled. What a terrible thing to happen to them. It wasn't the same as what had happened to her, but it was close. She had been used as an obsession, and they had been used for what they could do or buy.

The two women who had sung earlier joined them in the front of the salon. Apparently, they had heard Becca talk about Amelia.

"Those poor boys. Amelia ran them around in circles," said the dark haired woman. She appeared to be in her sixties. The other one nodded in agreement.

"Yep, Amelia always was a bad egg. Her father, bless his heart, never has been able to see that. He blamed Zach and Chase for not making his baby girl happy. No one could make her happy, even that rich man she married. Last time she came to visit, he looked downright miserable." The woman eyed Cassie speculatively. "Heard those boys are sweet on you."

Apparently, there were no secrets in a small town.

"Um, well, we're going to the drive-in tonight."

The first woman chuckled. "When I was young, we called it the Passion Pit. Why, I remember one night…well, never mind. It's hard to believe those boys are all grown-up. I remember when they were kids and giving their mother a hard time. Chase was so sweet and charming. He would be inside talking his mom out of a cookie before dinner. All the while, Zach was outside getting a ladder to climb up on the roof to set a trap for Santa Claus. I think he fell and broke his arm, too. Nancy was fit to be tied. Zach was the quiet, adventurous one. He didn't say much, unless something needed to be said. But he always got things done."

The other woman smiled at the memories.

"I remember when Chase started his own rock band. It's a good thing the Harper's didn't have any close neighbors. They were quite loud. Good, but loud. Chase has quite a voice."

"Chase can sing? I had no idea." Cassie marveled.

"Chase has an amazing voice. He can also play guitar, drums, and keyboards. He is an extremely accomplished musician. His band sang at my senior prom." Becca smiled at the memory.

The first woman chuckled. "I do remember that. Remember when Zach, Chase, Jack, and Sheriff Ryan hopped a Greyhound to Tampa when they were teenagers? They wanted to see a Buccaneers game. I think they were grounded for a month. Simply gave them more free time to think up their next escapade." The woman smiled at Becca. "Zach and Chase must seem like brothers to you. Thank goodness you never got caught up in their monkey shines."

Becca giggled. "Nope, I always had better sense than that. Although, I desperately wanted to be allowed into the fort they built one summer. But the rule was 'no girls allowed.' Still makes me mad thinking about that. I always wondered what they did in that fort."

The second woman rolled her eyes. "Probably read girlie magazines and had farting contests." She peered at Cassie. "Do you have family, dear?"

Cassie didn't really like to talk about her family, but she didn't want to be rude, either. "Yes, although my parents divorced when I was twelve. So I moved back and forth between them quite a bit."

Cassie didn't mention how her parents had remarried other people and each started new families. After that, they hadn't seemed very interested in their daughter. She must have been a reminder of their unhappy marriage. She had spent her teen years shuffling back and forth between her apathetic parents. She had found some solace in her friendship with Jillian. While Jillian's family life was far from idyllic, it had been a refuge where Cassie could find love and support from Jillian, and Jillian's mother and brother.

The woman tutted and shook her head. "Divorce is a nasty thing and hard on someone as young as you were. Well, you're in Plenty now, dear. We're all your family. And you can't get rid of your family."

* * * *

Zach waited impatiently in the front hall of their home. His brother better hurry the fuck up, or he was going to take the beautiful Cassie Ames out on a date and leave his brother's sorry ass at home to watch reruns on television. He had been looking forward to this date all week, and despite how busy he had kept himself, the days hadn't passed by quickly enough.

Zach smiled as he replayed the picnic in his mind. Cassie had finally relaxed around them, and they had enjoyed their time with her.

He was anxious to spend more time with her. She was not only beautiful and sexy but obviously intelligent and funny. She was the total package. In Zach's experience, the total package was damn near impossible to find.

He was at an age where he was ready to settle down and start a family. He was tired of going to bed and waking up alone. He wanted someone to share his life. He had grown up watching his parents' happy marriage, and he wanted the same. Amelia had soured their outlook on love for a while, but he was determined to put the past where it belonged. Cassie's arrival in Plenty was at just the right time. He wouldn't lose a chance with a woman like her due to fear.

He wanted to make sure that Cassie knew how much they really liked her and respected her, but it had been damn hard to be the gentleman at the picnic and not lean over and kiss her senseless and then some. He knew Chase, too, had struggled with his more primitive instincts that day. Cassie seemed to bring it out in both of them, but they would need to control themselves tonight so they didn't scare her off. Although beautiful, she didn't act as sophisticated about men as other women whom Zach had dated. And he had dated a lot of them over the years. In contrast, Cassie had seemed pretty shy. And hell, if she had ever dated two men who shared, he would be shocked. His brother running down the stairs interrupted his reverie.

"Mooning over her again?" Chase smirked.

"We both are, and you know it." Zach sighed. "We need to make sure we move slowly with Cassie tonight. I don't want us scaring her off. She's special. We can both see it. We just need to make her feel special. So don't go all caveman and fuckin' blow it. Got it, bro?"

"I'm not the one who goes all caveman, asshole. I believe that honor belongs to you more often than not. But, hell yeah, I got it. I don't want to scare Cassie, either. She blushed so much at the picnic, you would think she was a virgin."

"Well, if by some remote chance she is, she won't stay that way long with us around." Chase laughed as Zach punched him in the shoulder.

* * * *

Cassie knew she was in big trouble. When her two men—she couldn't help but think of them as her men—picked her up, she had almost fainted at how handsome they were. The heat had finally broken some, so they were both in button-down shirts and blue jeans that molded to their strong legs and highlighted two of the finest asses she had ever seen. They looked gorgeous, and she was glad she had taken extra time with her appearance. Her freshly trimmed hair was blown dry and loose around her shoulders. She had applied her makeup with a light hand and wore just a touch of perfume in a spot she swore these men wouldn't be seeing any time soon. It was still very warm when the sun was up, so she chose a flowered skirt which flared just above her knee and a lacy, black blouse that matched the edging on the skirt. Black, high-heeled sandals completed the outfit. She figured she would need the extra height with such tall men.

As they had driven onto Main Street, she had sat between their hard, warm bodies and inhaled their scents, and it had all but driven her insane. She had wanted Zach to pull the truck over and throw her body on top of theirs. What was wrong with her? She had never given sex a second thought before. Sex had never even been a priority or anything that she even particularly enjoyed, but with these men, she was completely obsessed. They would think she was a nympho and get a restraining order if she wasn't careful.

Now as she sat between them at Charlie's pizza parlor, she was trying to take deep breaths to relax her racing heart and fluttering pussy. She kept drying her sweaty palms on her flowered skirt and taking deep breaths. Hyperventilating was not in the plan tonight.

"So, what do you like on your pizza?" Zach asked with his dimpled smile. She almost choked on the sweet tea that Charlie had brought her. Damn, he was one fine man. And she only had to look a little to her right, and another fine man was sitting on the other side.

Well, wasn't she a lucky girl tonight.

"Lots of cheese, and Jillian and I usually have sausage. What do you guys have?"

Chase answered, "We're fine with sausage, sweetheart. Do you need more tea?" He looked around for Charlie, who seemed to appear from nowhere. Cassie guessed that Charlie was keeping a watchful eye on their date along with all the townspeople in the restaurant who seemed to be stealing glances at them every few seconds.

"So have y'all decided on what you are going to have tonight? The garlic bread sticks are coming out of the oven now, so I recommend those, of course. Will you be having your usual with everything?"

"Garlic bread sticks sound good, Charlie, and an extra-large pizza with sausage and double cheese. Also, Cassie needs some more tea when you have a minute," Zach said as he smiled affectionately at Charlie. Cassie could see that it was mutual and that these were good friends. She liked that. It made her feel safe knowing that people liked and respected Zach and Chase. It was important to her that she respected the man she was dating. Or, as she reminded herself, the two men she was dating.

"You know, if you guys normally have your pizza with everything, go ahead and order that on part of the pizza. I don't mind. Really." Cassie smiled at both the men. She was going to have to get used to talking and smiling to both of them equally. She didn't want to hurt anyone's feelings.

She liked both of them but in different ways already. Chase was the teaser and charmer. He liked to flirt and make her laugh. He connected to her with his words, wanting to find out every thought that went through her mind.

Zach was the intense and quiet one. He exuded hardness, but she could see the softness within. Zach connected to her by his attentiveness. He listened intently to whatever she had to say, his eyes focused on her. He moved his chair close and held her hand quietly, as if it calmed him to be so near to her. It certainly calmed her. She had never felt so safe.

"We're fine. We love Charlie's pizza no matter what it has on it, don't we, Chase?"

"Hell, yeah. Best pizza in the state of Florida. And her peanut butter pie isn't anything to sneeze at either."

Charlie left the table laughing and saying something about them being silver-tongued devils.

Cassie couldn't help herself. She wondered if her men had noticed all the attention they were getting from the other patrons. "Ummm…we seem to be getting a lot of attention from the other diners. I feel a little like a bear in the zoo."

Zach and Chase burst out laughing, and it was Chase who was able to answer first.

"Well, sweetheart, as long as they don't expect to watch us mate, I don't care. They can stare as much as they want. They aren't looking at me and Zach anyway. They're looking at how gorgeous you look tonight. You are probably the most beautiful woman in Plenty."

Cassie felt the heat in her cheeks at the sexual connotation, and Zach almost choked on his beer. "Angel, you are going to have to toughen up a little if you are going to take Chase's wicked sense of humor. He has never been known to be politically correct. Personally, I like your blushes, but with Chase's mouth, you are going to be walking around in a permanent state of embarrassment."

Cassie felt like she was already walking around in a permanent state of arousal since she had met these men. She gave them her best teacher stare and crossed her arms over her chest. The boys gulped and exchanged a quick glance. Then it was Cassie who burst into laughter. She was really having fun, and she realized that she hadn't had fun with a man in a very long time. Long past time, really. She needed to put the past behind her, and tonight was a good start.

She munched her garlic bread and listened to Zach and Chase tell a funny story about what had happened on a construction site that week. She didn't want to break the happy mood but felt compelled to ask them about their business.

"Have you had problems with your construction business with the economy the way it is?"

Zach looked thoughtful and then answered, "No, not really. There was no construction company in Plenty until we started ours. If you wanted something built, you called a company in a neighboring town. It was fine, but people here in Plenty like to patronize local businesses whenever they can. Plenty is still a growing town, so we pretty much have more business than we can handle. Chase and I just hired another crew, in fact. Of course, there is no telling how much more business we would have if the housing starts weren't way down. I'm glad to say that we're doing fine."

"Here's your pizza, folks." Charlie breezed over with their piping-hot pie and talked slowed down as they all dug into dinner.

Zach and Chase laughed as Cassie matched them slice for slice. Cassie was used to the attention regarding her appetite and just laughed and shrugged. "I have a very fast metabolism."

"Nothing wrong with that. Might want to save room for dessert, though. We brought snacks for the drive-in."

"I always have room for dessert, Zach."

Chapter 4

Chase couldn't remember a better evening. He had great pizza, lots of snacks, a scary movie on the big screen at the drive-in, and one sexy woman curled up between him and his brother. He glanced over at Zach and saw the same happiness that he felt reflected there. This was what they had been looking for—a smart, sassy woman who challenged them and still managed to be sweet and sexy all at the same time. Cassie was one hell of a woman, and he and Zach were lucky sons of bitches.

So far, neither one of them had come on too strong, but it was damn hard to hold his urges in check. The heat of her body and the scent of her skin seemed stronger in the close confines of the truck cab than they had in the pizza parlor. Each breath of her sweet scent, like spring and rain, sent blood pooling south, making his jeans damn uncomfortable.

He stared at her full lips and wondered how to make an opening to kiss her. He had hoped she would be so scared from the movie that she would be clinging to him and Zach, but as she had predicted, she was no wimp. At one point in the movie, she had actually called the heroine stupid for wearing high heels and was rooting for the monster to catch her and eat her. She might be a quiet little thing, but Cassie was a little bloodthirsty. He and Zach better watch their step around their woman.

Did I just call her "our woman"? What the hell?

"Geez, that woman is dumb! She deserves to be killed. She's doing Darwin a favor!"

Chase laughed, and Zach joined in at Cassie's outburst. She

seemed to be very frustrated with the heroine in the movie. "Are you laughing at me?" she demanded, pointing a finger at Zach's chest.

"No, ma'am," Zach laughed. "I am laughing right next to you."

"You better watch your step," Cassie's eyes narrowed. "I am learning a lot from this monster."

Chase laughed as Cassie tried to look mean, but it didn't quite come off.

"You better cool it, too, Chase. I won't be laughed at by a guy who jumped when the monster first appeared. I hope this movie isn't too scary for you."

Chase leaned forward and was almost nose to nose with Cassie. "No, ma'am, I am not too scared, and I did not jump when the monster appeared. I won't have you casting aspersions on my character, Miss Ames."

Cassie opened her mouth to reply but never got a chance. Chase took his opening and went in for the kiss he had been waiting for since the moment he met her.

* * * *

Cassie couldn't breathe. Chase's lips took hers softly, more softly than she expected. His lips were full and warm and soft. His tongue ran along the seam of her lips, and she opened up to his warmth. His tongue glided inside, and her heart raced even faster. Her tongue slid along his, and the world seemed to tilt.

Her hands climbed up his arms, over his broad shoulders, and around his neck. He lifted his lips for just a second to angle the kiss a little, and she caught her breath. Her eyes closed in ecstasy, and her head fell back as he continued to kiss her, more demanding now. He sucked at her tongue, and she could feel the flood of moisture from her pussy. Her panties were soaked, and Chase had only kissed her. Chase lifted his head and gave her a smile and turned her in his arms to her left. Confused for only a second, she realized that Chase was turning her to Zach.

"You look like a sexy angel. I can't wait to kiss you." Zach's voice was rougher than normal, and his eyes were a deeper blue than she had ever seen.

And then he was kissing her too. *These boys knew how to kiss!* Zach's lips were not as soft as Chase's, but they were just as exciting. Zach's kiss was more carnal and demanding, while Chase's more cajoling and romantic. Zach's tongue moved in and out of Cassie's mouth fucking her with his tongue. It showed exactly what Zach would like to be doing with another part of his anatomy.

Her pussy creamed and fluttered in response. She felt so empty, and only these men could fill the ache inside her. Her nipples were tight in response, and Chase must have noticed because she felt him slide his hands under her lace blouse. He began to kiss the back of her neck and ear while his fingers played over her lace-covered nipples.

Her mind began to short-circuit with so much stimulation, two sets of lips, four hands. *And two cocks!* She could feel Chase's impressive length pressed up against her back, and if she lowered her hands from Zach's chest just a little, she could have found out if he was just as hard as Chase.

When she thought she couldn't take any more pleasure, Zach lifted his head. His eyes were that deep blue, and he smiled slowly, showing off those dimples she had fantasized about kissing. This time, she gave in to temptation and reached up and traced them with her fingers and then boldly with her tongue.

"You're asking for trouble, angel," Zach growled, and Cassie's pussy dripped more honey in response to his masculine tone.

Chase turned Cassie back to him for another kiss, this one more passionate and demanding than the last. His fingers continued to pluck and caress her nipples, and she had no defense when he pulled the cups down and under her breasts. His fingers captured a nipple and gave a hard pinch, and Cassie cried out. Her nipples seemed to be directly connected to her clit, and it began to tingle and burn as she moved toward release. Her pussy clenched against the emptiness, needing something to fill her up to bring that release.

"Too rough, angel?" Zach asked.

"Yes…No…No, not too rough." Cassie spoke barely above a whisper and was surprised she could speak at all. Sensations swirled all around her, and she was lost to these two men who were quickly mastering her body.

"Good girl," Zach praised. "We want you to feel good. Let us take care of you."

Zach then slid his hand under Cassie's skirt and up over her lacy panties. His hand slid inside the panties and found her softness. She moaned as she felt his fingers glide through her folds. She was so wet, they slid easily. She caught her breath when his fingers grazed her swollen clit. She needed more.

* * * *

He needed to calm down. Zach's heart was beating so fast, and he was breathing so hard, he thought he might pass out from the pleasure. He had been fantasizing about it since he met her, and he was finally touching and stroking her. She felt hot and wet, and as his thumb found that little button of pleasure, he saw her head fall back and a moan escape from lips that were red and swollen from their kisses. He wanted to see how beautiful she was when she came. He wanted to see if she could handle his dark desires.

His cock was hard and aching as he listened to Cassie whimper and moan from Chase's fingers. He could probably pound nails with his dick, but he needed to concentrate on Cassie. Bring her pleasure and let her know that he and Chase weren't just fucking around with her. If they had been and she was a one-night stand, Zach would already be balls deep. Cassie was no one-night stand.

He locked eyes with Chase, and his brother seemed to get the unspoken message between them. Chase reached around and pulled

Cassie back into the cradle of his hips, facing Zach. Chase's hands were still under Cassie's lacy blouse, plucking her hard, pointed nipples. Cassie's eyes were closed in pleasure, and Chase leaned forward and captured her already swollen lips with his own.

Zach watched in satisfaction as Cassie writhed under the skillful hands of his brother. He had a few tricks of his own for Cassie, and his fingers slid back inside her panties again and slowly stroked her drenched slit. She was so wet, he had no problem sliding a finger inside her and swirling it around. Her hips bucked off the truck seat, but Chase had a hold of her and eased her back, all without breaking their kiss. Zach eased a second finger in and hooked his fingers a little, swirling them on a quest. She was tight, so tight and hot. Cassie's cry of pleasure as she tore her mouth from Chase's let Zach know he had found the sweet spot inside her. He continued to rub it while his thumb circled her clit. Her pussy clenched around him, and he knew she was close to release.

"She's close, Chase. Really close. If you want in on this, you better do it now."

* * * *

Cassie was on fire. She had never thought of herself as all that sexual, but these two men had her soaking her panties and on the edge of orgasm. Cassie watched, a little dazed, as Chase rearranged himself so that one hand could reach inside her panties along with Zach's.

"I do want in on this, brother. Did you find it?"

"Yep, slide in here and let me show you."

Cassie cried out again with the pleasure as Chase slid a finger inside her next to Zach's two. "Shhh, sweetheart. Just hold still for a minute while you get used to me and Zach inside you."

Cassie wanted to tell them that she hadn't cried out from pain but from pleasure, but her vocal chords weren't working, and then Chase started to move his finger, and she lost all thought as he also found her sweet spot and rubbed it softly. Zach's thumb circled her clit. She felt the earth spinning and tilting as something tightened inside of her. She was so close, but she couldn't seem to get there. She mewled in frustration and bucked her hips again.

"Easy there, Cassie. Just let go. Give us your pleasure." Zach picked up the pace with his fingers.

"Come on, sweetheart. You look so sexy for us. Give us one, Cassie." Chase kept rubbing the sweet spot inside her as Cassie began to writhe and moan, stretched between them. The frustration of release just being out of her reach was maddening. She twisted in their arms, but they easily held her down.

Through her haze of pleasure, Cassie heard Zach's deep, commanding voice, "Come now, Cassie. Do it now."

At his dark tone, Cassie threw back her head as the world went blindingly white. She vaguely heard someone cry out, and she realized that it was her making that sound. Her body spasmed with the pleasure, and it seemed to go on and on forever. She rode their fingers all the way down to earth, and finally, she lay between them panting, spent, and drained. She opened her eyes slowly to see Zach and Chase smiling tender smiles at her.

"That sure looked like fun, sweetheart." Chase grinned at her.

"Yeah, you sure are beautiful when you come, angel." Zach gently pulled his fingers from her sensitive pussy, and she watched in shock as he began to lick them clean. "Damn, you taste good. Next time, I am going to lick and kiss that pussy so you come again and again for me."

Cassie was still dazed but finally found her voice. "I don't think I could survive again and again. I barely survived that one."

Zach and Chase laughed as they pulled her up in their arms and cuddled her between them, kissing her face, lips, neck, and any other exposed skin.

Zach tucked a stray lock of hair behind her ear. "You'll get used to it, Cassie. We are going to make you come over and over again and give you pleasure like you have never known. You will give us the same pleasure."

Cassie wasn't so sure. She had never had much luck with sex. No man had ever told her she was great in bed or anything. How was she supposed to keep two gorgeous, sexy men satisfied?

Chase's finger tapped her nose with a grin. "No frowning, sweetheart. Let's get you put back together and watch the rest of the movie."

Chase began straightening her clothes while Zach opened a bottle of water for her. How did he know she was thirsty? She had never known men who were so attentive to her needs before.

As she gratefully accepted the water, she couldn't help but notice the very large bulge in Zach's jeans. One glance to her right told her that Chase was in the same state. It didn't seem right that they had taken such good care of her and now had to be, well…uncomfortable was probably not too strong a word.

"Uh…guys…can I…um…take care of you?" She let her hands trail down their chests toward their straining erections. She wasn't ambidextrous, but she would give it a try.

They both caught her hands before she got to her destination.

"Not this time, Cassie. We wanted to give you pleasure tonight. We'll be fine. Don't tell any of your girlfriends because men don't like this to get out, but a case of blue balls won't kill us." Zach grinned, and she could see the dimples that she loved so much.

"I won't tell anyone. I wouldn't want you to get in trouble from the Secret Society of Sexy Men."

"Sexy men, huh? I like the sound of that." Chase grinned and leaned back on the truck seat.

"I am sure you two haven't had much trouble attracting the opposite sex," Cassie said with a roll of her eyes.

Chase laughed at Cassie's expression. "No way are you going to get us talking about other women when we're with you. But, we don't date around. While we are dating you, we won't be dating anyone else. You can count on that. We're not kids anymore, and we know how to respect a woman."

Cassie was shocked at his straightforward honesty. This was far from her experience with men.

"I appreciate your honesty and respect. I'm not really used to it. I haven't had the best luck with men."

That's an understatement.

Zach's gaze was intense and direct when he spoke to her. "Men in Plenty respect women, angel. You best get used to being treated that way."

Chapter 5

Cassie sipped her wine and recounted the evening to Jillian and Becca. It was their girls-night-in.

"They really said that? What the fuck? And they promised you an exclusive relationship?" Jillian looked amazed.

Becca answered for her. "Yep, the men in Plenty respect women. They don't run around behind a woman's back. That's not how they're raised."

Becca laughed at Jillian's shocked expression.

"Boy, are the men here different than Chicago. No man there would ever be caught dead expressing a feeling that he wouldn't fuck around or tell a girl that she wasn't a casual relationship. It kind of freaks me out a little. Does anyone do casual?"

Cassie knew that Jillian was terrified of anything that even came close to commitment. Cassie and Jillian had dated many men in Chicago. Cassie had always been looking for Mr. Right, someone she could have a real family with. Jillian, on the other hand, didn't want to get serious. She just wanted to have fun. When a guy got serious, Jillian dumped him, and Cassie never saw the poor bastard again.

She knew Jillian had good reason to be scared. Jillian's parents had been pretty much miserable every single day of their marriage. Her father had cheated on her mom for years. Jillian had been caught in the middle of their tug-of-war and always swore that she would never live like that again.

Becca shrugged her shoulders and poured more wine into their glasses. "Yes, but everyone knows it up front."

Cassie shook her head and took a large gulp of wine. "I need to move slowly. I've made mistakes in the past with men. I don't want a repeat."

"Dated some losers, huh? We all have I think," Becca said sympathetically.

Cassie stared at the ceiling thinking about the past. "Well, one loser in particular. I used to date a lot. I liked to go out and have fun. Jillian and I have had some epic double-dates."

Jillian laughed at the memories. "Oh yeah, remember the one guy who wanted all his food on separate plates? He didn't want his food to touch."

Becca frowned. "I don't like my food to touch."

Jillian shook her head. "I don't either, but this guy took it to the limit. He brought his own silverware and ate his food clockwise."

Becca's eyes went wide. "Ohhh, he sounds…well, weird as shit, Jillian."

"He was. My brother, Mark, introduced me to him as a joke. Mark has a wicked sense of humor."

Cassie giggled as she remembered how they had gotten their revenge. "We got him back though. We put BENGAY in his boxers. I swear, he chased us around the entire neighborhood. Do you remember the guy I dated that constantly had to high-five every one? Or the guy that you dated that had an unnaturally close relationship with his mother?"

Jillian doubled over in laughter, tears running from her eyes.

"Oh shit. I think we have drunk too much wine, eaten too much cheesecake, and told Becca way too much."

Becca joined in the laughter. "You guys haven't cornered the market on strange dates. Have you ever been on a double-date with your brother? We'd be out to dinner, and Jack would suddenly yell 'hand check' to make sure my date hadn't put his hands anywhere near me. I was so embarrassed, I could have dug a hole and crawled in it."

Jillian nodded in agreement. "Brothers can be so protective. Mark still asks me about my boyfriends and offers to do background checks on them. I worked for the Public Defender office in Chicago. I could have done a background check myself. Mark's great, though. I couldn't ask for a better brother. Although, that stunt with the BENGAY got Cassie and I grounded for a week."

Cassie huffed indignantly. "She wasn't even my mom, and she grounded me."

Not that my mom paid enough attention to ground me.

Becca was puzzled. "Why didn't your mom ground you? Why did Jillian's mom do it?"

Cassie felt her heart ache a little. Suddenly, she was that teenage girl trying to get her mother's attention. She had never succeeded.

"I'm not really all that close to my family. I spent most of my teenage years at Jillian's house. I just exchange cards at the holidays with my family."

"That's so sad!" Becca looked heartbroken for her. "I can't imagine not being close to my dad and brothers. And of course, Zach and Chase are like brothers, too. They hung out with Ryan and Jack pretty much all the time. I miss my Mom, too. She was wonderful."

"You're lucky. My mom just wasn't the motherly type, even with her other children. She married money and had a nanny raise the kids."

Sometimes, Cassie wondered if things might have turned out differently if she had a mother's wisdom and guidance. Would she have met men like Zach and Chase earlier?

"We're getting too maudlin. Let's get to the good stuff. How was the sex last night?" Jillian asked waggling her eyebrows.

"I did not have sex with them! I just…well…we started kissing and…" Cassie stammered and felt her face getting red.

"Oooo…you're blushing. That's a good sign. Obviously, more than a kiss, but less than sex. Hmm…Are they as good as they look?"

Cassie sighed and rolled her eyes. "Oh god. They are better than they look. I have never felt that way before. It was like nothing I have ever experienced. And well, two sets of lips, two tongues, four hands…unbelievable."

"I am so damn jealous, I could just spit, Cassie Ames. If you weren't my friend, I would have to hate you."

"Seems to me, Jillian, that you could have a couple men any time you wanted to. Becca's brothers sure seem interested."

Cassie and Becca laughed at Jillian's outraged expression. Apparently, Jillian didn't want to talk about it. "Let's get the subject back to you, my friend. Did you tell them about Danny?"

Cassie's grew serious at Jillian's question. "Who's Danny?" Becca asked.

Cassie's lips tightened in distaste. "We'll need more wine if you want to hear that story. And no, Jillian, I was enjoying myself so much, I didn't want to ruin the evening. We came here for a fresh start, and I don't want the specter of Danny Trent ruining my happiness. He doesn't get to fucking win. I refuse to carry around this baggage for the rest of my life."

"Everyone has baggage, Cass. Yours just has a name and a prisoner identification number."

* * * *

Danny Trent leaned back on the bunk of his cell and stared at the picture taped to the bottom of the upper bunk. The paper was starting to yellow and was looking worn from his fingers. It was the only thing in this fucking cell he cared about, and he wondered if he could sneak it out when they transferred him in a few weeks.

Danny's eyes narrowed as he stared at the blonde in the picture and blew out the breath he was holding. The picture was from the media coverage of his trial, and it didn't do Cassandra justice. He liked to call her Cassandra. Other people called her Cassie, but she would always be Cassandra to him. He was special to her, so he got to call her a special name.

He heard from a friend at the accounting firm that Cassandra had quit her job and moved to some small town in Florida. He wondered what she was doing right now and if she thought of him. He thought about her every day. Cassandra belonged to him, but she didn't seem to understand that. She kept pushing him away. That would never do. She needed to understand that she belonged to him and should behave that way. He didn't want to have to punish her again. He hated when he had to punish her. But if she continued to defy and disrespect him, he had no choice. He remembered his father telling him that women were whores and sluts until they found the right man to make them behave. Then they needed to obey that man or be punished.

Danny knew that he just needed to be patient. Eventually, he would have the opportunity to get out of this hellhole. He was going to be a model prisoner. They were already calling him rehabilitated. Fuck yeah. And then, when he got his chance, he would find Cassandra and reunite with his one true love.

* * * *

"We should have sent flowers, bro."

Zach sighed and looked at his brother's determined expression. They had had this conversation a couple of times already, and apparently, they were going to have it again. Perhaps he could cut this conversation short by changing the subject.

"I promise next time we will send flowers, okay? Is Ryan joining us, too?" Zach pushed open the door of their favorite watering hole and was hit by a blast of loud rock music that rattled his teeth. They had been meeting Jack and Ryan every week for a beer since they were old enough to drink. Legally, anyway. The only exception had been when Zach was in the Middle East. Even then, Chase had kept up the tradition.

"Yeah, both he and Jack are off duty tonight. Doesn't Ryan owe us a round since he lost that football bet?"

Zach grinned as he remembered the bet that Ryan had argued was a sure thing. He should know by now that college football was too unpredictable. He should also know better than to bet against the Gators.

Zach spied Jack and Ryan at a table near the back. Zach led Chase through the maze of tables in the dimly lit bar, narrowly escaping being nailed by a falling beer bottle. The band onstage was doing a loud, but pretty decent cover of a Led Zeppelin song. Zach pulled out a chair and sank gratefully into it. It had been a long day at the construction site. "Looks like you started without us."

Jackson Parks lifted his beer in a salute. "We just got here. Ordered a bucket of beers. On good old Ryan, of course. So help yourself."

The men laughed, and Ryan rolled his eyes. "I would have won that bet if the running back hadn't pulled his hamstring. You got lucky, Zach."

"Luck has nothing to do with it. I simply analyzed the two teams, looked at all the variables including weather and field condition, and made what I consider to be an educated call."

Jack snorted. "You are so full of shit. You guessed."

"Doesn't really matter, does it? Ryan's buying."

Zach leaned back in his chair and scanned the crowd. Evaluating his surroundings and the people around him were habits leftover from his SEAL days. It had saved his life or someone else's more than once.

"See any troublemakers, buddy? As the sheriff, I'm authorized to arrest them."

Jackson piped in too. "As a firefighter, I am trained by Homeland Security to deal with any mayhem they may be planning."

Chase rolled his eyes. "Don't encourage him. Last week, Zach wouldn't let me sell a horse to a guy that had, and I quote, non-standard body language. Shit."

Zach took a long draw on his beer. "You know, guys, I know over one hundred ways to kill a man. I'm thinking of a few of them right now."

"I know a few myself." Ryan smirked.

Leo, the bartender, walked up to the table and slapped Chase on the back. "Gonna give us a song or two tonight, Chase? I know my customers would love it."

"I've had a long day, Leo. I think I'll pass tonight."

"C'mon, Chase. We haven't heard you sing for a long time. Join in tonight," Jack cajoled.

Chase shook his head. "No. I'm just not in the mood to sing tonight. Maybe next time."

Leo looked disappointed. "Well, if you change your mind, we'd love to hear you tonight, especially if you've written anything new lately. I'll be behind the bar if you change your mind."

Ryan caught Zach's eye as Leo headed back to the front of the bar. Ryan was the only person in the world who knew how guilty he felt that Chase hadn't followed his dream into the music business. Chase had been given a chance to join a band and go on the road. That was the same time that Zach had been given his orders for deployment overseas. Chase had given up the opportunity to stay in Plenty and take care of the horse farm. That band had recently signed a recording contract.

Zach often wondered if Chase regretted his decision. Zach asked Chase about it once, and he had just laughed and said he never really wanted to leave Plenty, and he didn't have enough talent anyway. Zach hoped that Chase was telling the truth. What he did know was that Chase had taken on a great deal of responsibility when Zach left to serve his country. It was true the saying that the families of service personnel make sacrifices, too.

The new waitress brought them a fresh bucket of beers. Zach's limit was one tonight. It was his turn to drive. He asked her quietly if she could bring him a Coke.

"Like what you see there, Jack?" Chase followed Jack's wolfish gaze. The waitress had lush curves and long, dark hair.

"Hell, yeah. Maybe you and I should introduce ourselves to the new waitress." Jack elbowed Ryan in the ribs.

Ryan just shook his head. "I prefer redheads."

Chase pounced on his statement. "You wouldn't be hankering after Cassie's best friend would you? She is cute, if you like redheads."

Jackson sat straight up in his chair and scowled. "Yes, he does like the new teacher. And it's ruining all my fun, dammit. What's so special about this girl anyway?"

Zach was surprised. "You haven't met Jillian yet? She's a sweet girl."

"Sweet? I suppose she's fun and smart, too," Jack said snarkily.

Ryan's eyes narrowed at his younger brother. Zach knew that look. If he wasn't careful, Jack was going to get his ass kicked.

"What the fuck is wrong with sweet, fun, and smart? I'm sick of dating girls that are only in it for the kinky sex. I'm thirty-two years old. Sleeping around ceased to be fun a long time ago. Grow up, Jack. And anyway, Jillian is gorgeous. We should be so lucky to have a woman like her."

Zach nodded in agreement. "It's time to settle down and stop fucking around. My parents were married and had three kids by now. Don't you want a family, Jack?"

Jack shrugged. "Sure I do. But I haven't met a woman yet who made me think about marriage and kids."

A smile played around Ryan's lips. "You haven't met Jillian yet. I felt like someone punched me in the stomach the first time I saw her. And we have the same taste in women, bro. Just like Chase and Zach do. Sorry, you're a goner, man."

Jack's shoulders slumped. "Well, I had a good run while it lasted, I guess. Is she really gorgeous? She's not like Amelia is she?"

Ryan rolled his eyes. "Yes, she is gorgeous, and fuck no, she is not like Amelia. I've only seen her a few times, and I can tell that."

Chase ran a hand over his face as if to rub away the bad memories. "No one is like Amelia. That witch is in a class all by herself."

Jack chuckled. "She's by herself because no one wants to be anywhere near her. That woman is toxic."

Zach nodded grimly. That was a good description of Amelia. "I don't want our time with Amelia to color our relationship with Cassie. Cassie is completely different. I don't know what we ever saw in Amelia."

Ryan's eyebrows rose. "You don't? I seem to remember nonstop, kinky, sweaty sex being the main attraction. I'm surprised your dicks didn't fall off. Does Cassie know about your past exploits? Might want to tell her."

Zach shook his head. "No, she doesn't know our history, and frankly, that is probably just as well. She would think we were a couple of jerks out for a piece of ass. She's no piece of ass."

Chase waved a hand toward the crowded bar. "Hate to break it to you, bro, but I am guessing the entire town has filled her in on our exploits by now. No sense regretting or apologizing for it at this point. If she asks, we just tell her it is all in the past—which it damn well is, anyway."

"I guess your date last night went well then?" Jack asked.

Zach could see Chase's eyes go a little dreamy. "Yeah, it went great. Cassie's a sweetheart. Smart, funny, and down-to-earth."

Chase gave Jack a look. "Sexy as hell, too. A woman a man can be proud to be with. I imagine Jillian is the same."

Jack raised his hands in surrender. "I get it. I'm an ass, okay? So when are you going to see Cassie again?"

"We invited her over for dinner tomorrow night. Zach and I are going to grill some steaks. Show her how domesticated we are."

Jackson almost choked on his beer. "Yeah, you guys are just like kittens. Just try not to give her food poisoning. That usually ruins the romantic vibe."

Zach leaned back in his chair with a big grin. "Nothing is going to ruin the mood. Everything with Cassie is going to be great."

* * * *

"How do you like your steak, Cassie?"

Cassie reclined on the lounge chair beside the pool and Jacuzzi. Zach looked very at home grilling their steaks in the fancy, outdoor kitchen. Zach had explained that he and Chase had just finished building the house and had spoiled themselves a little with some "boy's toys." They certainly had. The living room was decked out with butter-soft leather couches and an enormous flat-screen TV with surround sound. One end of the room had a piano, a drum set, and a couple of guitars littering the carpet. Her tour of their home had also included their office, where the toys continued. Each man had his own dark oak desk with a giant leather chair and state-of-the-art computer equipment and another large flat-screen on the wall. The boys liked their comforts, apparently.

"Medium rare, Zach. And might I say, it is a fine sight watching a handsome man cook for me. I could get used to this."

"Might not want to get too used to it. Grilling is about all Chase and I can do when it comes to food. We were hoping you could cook, honestly."

Zach laughed, and Cassie's body began to hum at the rich sound. He looked so yummy standing there in his worn blue jeans that hugged that very fine ass and a red T-shirt that stretched across his broad chest and biceps. Yep, that man had some guns on him. For the first time in her life, Cassie could see why women appreciated a man that did physical labor for a living. She would bet that Zach didn't get that body by spending hours in a gym.

"Will Chase be back by dinner?"

"Yeah, he should be. He needed to head down to the stables to check on a horse that should foal any day now."

"You didn't go with him?"

"Chase and I don't go everywhere with each other, Cassie, although it might look otherwise to you since we started courting you. Actually, Chase is much better with the horses that are foaling. Almost like that horse whispering guy. He has a real soft touch with them. I, on the other hand, am the designated asshole on our construction sites, and no one accuses me of whispering." Zach grinned and showed Cassie those gorgeous dimples she loved so much. Hmmm, she would have to get a taste of those later.

"The designated asshole? I'm afraid to ask, but what is that?"

"The designated asshole is the guy that yells if someone needs yelled at, rips someone a new asshole if they need a new one ripped, and generally terrorizes those that might want to screw around instead of working. Sort of like good cop, bad cop, angel. But Chase is bad cop, and I am even badder cop." Zach's eyes twinkled, and Cassie wondered if he was serious.

"Really, you yell at people? You seem like a pretty calm guy to me." Cassie really couldn't imagine Zach pissed off at all.

"Nope, actually Chase yells. I get silent and cold. I have been told that is even scarier. Learned to do that in the military."

"I heard you were in the Navy. Were you overseas?"

"Yep, I did two tours in Afghanistan. I was a Navy SEAL." Zach looked away a little embarrassed.

"Oh my god, you mean like the SEALs that got Bin Laden, SEALs?"

Zach really did look embarrassed now. "Yeah. I did covert missions for four years over there. Don't ask me about them, I would have to kill you if I told you."

Cassie looked startled at that and then busted out laughing as she saw Zach was grinning ear to ear. "What a kidder! I actually would like to hear about your missions, Zach. Was it dangerous?"

Zach was quiet a minute and seemed far off. Then just as suddenly, he turned back to her with an intense stare. "I don't really talk about it much, angel. It's in the past, and that's where it needs to stay," Zach said quietly, but firmly.

Cassie could tell that she wasn't going to hear heroic tales from the Middle East from Zach. She could see that it was a serious subject for him. Perhaps, one day, Zach would feel comfortable enough to talk to her about it. It explained his intensity and the aura of power that he radiated. That she was so attracted to a man that screamed "alpha" was completely unforeseen. Perhaps it was okay since his dominance was tempered with Chase's playful, romantic nature. Maybe she could get Chase to sing her a romantic song.

Zach definitely put out the "I am completely in charge" vibe, and she found herself responding to it. It surprised her. She had always been the one in charge in her past relationships, not counting Danny. And she would not think about Danny tonight. She was determined to move beyond her past. It had defined her long enough. "Well, then let's change the subject. So, you two are courting me, are you? I don't think I have ever been courted before. Not sure what I am supposed to do." Cassie giggled at Zach's eye roll when she mentioned courting.

"You don't have to do anything except sit back and let Chase and I take care of your every little need."

"All my needs, Zach?"

"Every single one. In fact, let's take care of one now."

And with that, Zach stalked toward her like the predator he was. He crawled up the lounge chair, and Cassie couldn't help but try to back up. He looked scary handsome and more than a little dangerous. Dangerous to her libido. Dangerous to her independence.

Zach was having none of that. He caught her by the ankle and tugged her toward him. "Nope, Cassie. You are about to get kissed. I've been thinking about this since Friday night."

Zach tugged Cassie into his arms and pushed her back on the lounge chair. She sucked in a breath as he leaned in and gently took her lips with his own. She had been thinking about this, too, since Friday night. She opened to him without hesitation, and he sucked her tongue into his mouth. God, he tasted good—just a hint of beer and something spicy she couldn't identify.

Zach lifted his head briefly to angle his kiss, and Cassie's heart beat faster as she caught the carnal need and lust in his eyes. He wasn't bothering to hide how he felt, and she knew without a doubt that Zach wanted her. And, God, did she want him badly, too. Her nipples had peaked against her lacy bra and were begging for Zach's fingers and tongue.

Her pussy was weeping with need and felt so empty. Her body remembered Zach's mastery of it and wanted more. Zach's kiss deepened, and Cassie ran her hands up his muscled back to his broad shoulders. She just couldn't resist running her fingers through his dark hair, and as she did, his lips traveled across her cheek to her ear, then down her jaw and neck to the swell of her breasts. His tongue snaked out and ran under her blouse to the edging of her bra. Cassie's head fell back as his tongue was oh-so-close to her nipples. They hardened to painful points as they begged for Zach's tongue to swirl across them, suck at them. She whimpered a little, and Zach's mouth closed over hers again, plundering her hot depths over and over again with his tongue.

Need swirled through her, and she could hear her ragged breath when Zach raised his head and rubbed his stubbly cheek on her smooth one. Her body jolted in reaction to his maleness, and she couldn't help her hips lifting toward his and felt his hard length against her. She felt him slowly lifting away with a groan he didn't bother to hide. She opened her eyes to see his wry smile.

"We better slow down or dinner is going to burn. But let's hold this thought for after dinner."

Zach pulled her up next to him, and she smiled at him as he looked at her through heavy-lidded eyes that spoke of his need.

"All right, Zach, but those steaks better be damn good."

Chapter 6

Zach propped his feet up on the coffee table as Cassie snuggled a little closer to him on the couch. Dinner had been great, and Cassie had seemed very appreciative of the steaks, corn on the cob, garlic bread, and chocolate brownies—courtesy of the neighborhood bakery. Chase had turned on the Sunday night football game and had Cassie's feet in his lap, giving them a massage. He could see Cassie's eyes close. Chase had found a particularly sensitive spot on her arch.

"Like that, baby? I can rub these cute little feet all night if you want."

"Oh man, that feels so good. I wear heels all week at school and my feet get so sore. Your hands are magic."

"You have no idea, sweetheart." Chase waggled his eyebrows suggestively and made Cassie laugh.

"Keep it up, Chase. Cassie is melting in a little puddle on my lap. I think you found a couple of sensitive spots on her that we need to catalog for the future."

Cassie giggled, and Zach smiled. He loved to hear his girl laugh, so he was surprised when Cassie pulled her feet from Chase and sat up on the couch with a serious look on her face. She had been quiet since they finished dinner.

"Guys, I need to talk to you about something. It's important, or I wouldn't bring it up. If we are going to be in a relationship, there is something you need to know."

Zach gave Chase a worried look. He picked up the remote and turned off the TV so they could give Cassie their undivided attention. He saw Cassie steady herself and take a deep breath. Whatever it was she wanted to say, it didn't look too easy for her.

"I need to tell you what brought me to this town. Why I left Chicago and came here."

They thought she had come to town for a change from city life. Was there something else?

"I came to town because I got fired from my job."

Zach gave Cassie a gentle look and stroked her hand.

"That's okay, Cassie. No one cares that you got fired." Chase looked at Zach in relief, but Zach knew there was more to this. He didn't feel relief yet. His instincts from his SEAL days were telling him this story was far from over, and none too pleasant. He saw Cassie tighten her lips as if she was about to say something really unpleasant. He braced himself for words he didn't want to hear.

"I got fired because of my stalker." Cassie's eyes darted back and forth between the brothers as he saw she was waiting for them to react.

What the fuck?

Chase hopped up from the couch and looked ready to do battle.

"Sit down, Chase. Let Cassie finish." He hoped he sounded a hell of a lot more calm than he felt. If someone had hurt Cassie…well, he didn't want to think about what he might have to do. Primitive instinct was washing through him to protect his woman, and he had to tamp it down so she could finish her story. He gripped her hand and looked deep into her stormy-blue eyes. He had never seen them look this gray before, as if her thoughts were making them cold, too.

"First, he isn't stalking me anymore, so you can sit down, Chase." Cassie looked pointedly at Chase, who had taken up pacing back and forth in the living room. Chase paused and took a deep breath as if to calm himself down.

"My stalker is in jail and, hopefully, will stay there for the next five years, although I am told he will probably only serve two if he has good behavior. His name is Danny Trent. I met him at the accounting firm where I worked. I was an accountant in Chicago and he was our IT consultant. He was always in and out of the office, and I thought I knew him well. He seemed like a pretty nice guy. He was always flirting with me and eventually asked me out. We went to a movie and had dinner, and honestly, something seemed off about the guy. Kind of creepy, you know. There was a table of guys next to us, and he kept saying that they were coming on to me. They never said a word to me, and I don't think they even looked my way. I think they were into each other, if you know what I mean. He dropped me at my house, I kissed him good night, and he started talking about us going away for the weekend and meeting his family. And it wasn't so much what he was saying as the way he said it. He was so determined. I ducked into the house not realizing that my life was not going to be the same again. Ever."

He gave Chase a look, and they each sat close and held her, letting her find the words. She finally spoke again.

"I wouldn't go out with Danny again. He kept calling, and I kept turning him down. He sent flowers, dropped gifts off at the office and my apartment building, and hung out wherever I was. It was creepy, but at that time, not scary, more of a nuisance than anything. Most of my friends made jokes about it calling him my Not So Secret Admirer or Cassie's Fan Club of One, stuff like that. Only Jillian seemed to really see him for what he was. She's like that, you know. She can see to a person's soul in less than a minute."

Zach hated to ask this next question, but he had to. "And what was Danny Trent, Cassie?"

Cassie looked up at him with the most heartbroken eyes he had ever seen and whispered softly, "He was evil. Pure evil."

* * * *

Cassie knew she needed to get her emotions under control, but telling the story brought so many feelings back that she thought she had conquered. She had started the evening with the idea she would never tell them about Danny. Now she knew that if they were going to have a relationship, she needed them to know her story. These men were worth walking through hell just one more time. She needed to bury the past once and for all.

"I thought Danny would eventually lose interest, but instead, things escalated. He began to harass my friends for information about me. He called all day and all night. I had to change my phone number several times. Jillian and I moved twice, but he always seemed to find me, and he would be even more agitated when he did.

"He broke into my apartment and took personal items, lingerie, books, CDs, perfume, stuff like that. One day, he broke in and had masturbated on my bed with my panties. The police couldn't arrest him because they had no proof it was him, just my say-so. My calls were being recorded, I had a restraining order, but he kept escalating and getting sicker every day." Cassie's voice shook as she remembered the horrible afternoon she had come home and found her bed and privacy violated.

"Shhh, Cassie. Chase and I are here for you. We aren't going to let anything happen to you ever again." Zach and Chase were running their hands up and down her back and arms, trying to soothe her, but Cassie knew the worst was yet to come.

"I was constantly scared, and Jillian wouldn't let me go anywhere by myself, and the police agreed. Danny seemed unhinged and capable of anything. I wasn't sleeping or eating, and Jillian was a wreck too. We moved again, and things seemed fine for a while. We had moved in the middle of the night, and the apartment we rented was in Jillian's brother's name. We thought we had gotten away this time. But...but..." Cassie paused, taking a deep breath as she remembered the horrific sight that had greeted her and Jillian when they got home from work one day.

Zach and Chase continued to stroke and pet her and tried to speak soothing words. How could she describe such ugliness to them?

"Jillian had picked me up from work, and we came home and

found…found…" Cassie tried to take several deep breaths. She had to get the rest of the story out.

"Danny had broken into our apartment and killed my dog, Dillon—snapped his neck. Dillon was a gift from Jillian when we moved to the new apartment, sort of a fresh start kind of thing. I have always loved dogs and hadn't had one for a few years. Dillon was just a puppy. That asshole killed my baby!"

Cassie threw herself at Zach's solid chest and sobbed. She sobbed for the loss of Dillon, for the loss of her innocence that day. She had found out then that evil lived in this world, and no one was immune from it. Evil wore many faces. Some of them were handsome, but that didn't make them less dangerous.

* * * *

Chase looked at Zach in horror. He couldn't believe what Cassie was telling them. That something like this had happened to her wanted to make him howl in frustration that he wasn't there to protect her. He knew that Zach felt the same. They would protect this woman with their lives. She had already been through too much.

Chase held Cassie as she purged tears that he thought had probably been a long time coming. She tried to be strong, but this was a horror that no one should face alone. Thank God, her friend Jillian had been there.

As Cassie calmed down, Chase handed her a tissue and pulled her on his lap, stroking her hair.

"The police arrested Danny, but he got out on bail a few hours later. However, they were supposed to call me if he made bail, but there was a clerical snafu, and the paperwork didn't get where it should have. I didn't know he got out. I was out alone since I thought he was in jail. He found me in the parking garage of the mall."

Chase held Cassie tighter, afraid to hear what had happened when this asshole had found her.

"He was so angry and was yelling at me about disobeying him and disrespecting him. To this day, I really don't know what he was talking about. Anyway, he grabbed my hair and pushed me down to my knees. He said he wanted me to beg and beg loudly so that everyone would know who I belonged to. When I wouldn't beg, he started to slap and punch me, kick me while he held my hair tightly."

Cassie paused, and Chase felt sick as he saw how pale her face was and how gray her eyes had become.

"Luckily, there were police patrolling the mall parking garage. They came upon the scene by accident, but they caught him in the act this time. They arrested him, and he didn't get bail that time. The next eight months were a blur of statements, lawyers, pre-trial motions, the actual trial, and the sentencing. When it was over, Danny Trent was sentenced to five years for assault, stalking, and cruelty to animals. My asshole employers decided that the publicity from the trial was bad for business. So once the trial was over, they fired me. And here I am...I just wanted you guys to know that I come with baggage. This started two years ago, and I haven't been on a date since that night with Danny Trent."

Cassie looked at each of them in turn as she stroked their cheeks. Chase tried to be calm but felt the rage hot inside him that anyone would dare hurt their woman. Yeah, that's right, he said it. Their woman. He wouldn't let the past, hers or theirs, stand in the way of happiness.

He just wanted ten minutes with this Danny Trent guy. He wanted to heal the hurt that Cassie had experienced. He wanted to erase the horror.

Chase knew they both looked devastated by what she had said, but that they needed to stay calm for her sake. "Sweetheart, no one will ever hurt you again, I can promise you. Zach and I protect and care for what is ours."

"That's right, angel. We feel special that you trust us this much. Trust us to be the first men you have dated in so long. We won't betray that trust, Cassie. You mean too much to us."

Chase saw Cassie finally smile. The crying had been good for their woman. She looked like a weight had been lifted from her shoulders.

"Yes, boys, I know you will take care of me. I can tell you are good men because I have seen evil, and you two aren't even close." Cassie grinned at the men. "That's why I want you to do something for me."

"What?" Both Zach and Chase spoke at the same time, eager to do anything to make Cassie happy.

"I want you to make love to me, boys, please."

Yes, ma'am, Chase thought, and he could see Zach grinning, too. Yep, a little sexual healing. That's what Cassie needed, and he and Zach would be the ones to give it to her.

Chapter 7

Zach leaned down to scoop Cassie into his arms and headed for the bedroom.

"Zach! Put me down! I can walk, you know."

Zach laughed. "I am well aware that you can walk, angel. But I like carrying you. Is that a problem? Besides, Chase and I aren't taking any chances that you'll change your mind and make a run for it."

Zach felt Cassie's giggle against his chest. "No chance that I will change my mind. I'm all yours tonight."

He and Chase exchanged a look. They hoped she really meant that. They were certainly all hers. In a matter of a few dates, she had managed to become incredibly important to both of them.

Her intelligence, sense of humor, and innate goodness called to him as no woman ever had. Her story tonight had touched a part of him he didn't often acknowledge. He knew about hell up close and personal after his time in the Middle East. Her goodness healed the hole in him that had gnawed away at his gut since he came home. He wanted to heal her, too. Perhaps together, with Chase's help, they could become whole.

He was falling in love with her, and he had no intention of fighting it. If anything, he welcomed the feeling. He was sure Chase did, too. They were at the point in their lives when they were ready for Cassie Ames and for love.

Chase flipped on the side lamp, and Zach gently dumped Cassie on his bed. He quickly came down over her, effectively trapping her underneath him with an arm on each side of her. His heart was pounding in his chest, and his skin seemed to have come to life wherever Cassie touched him. She was stroking his biceps and up over his shoulders, leaving a trail of tingling as she went.

He couldn't believe how nervous he was at that moment. He had been with many women over the years on his own and with Chase. No woman affected him the way Cassie did. She had his heart all twisted up and the rest of his body, too. She was probably half his size, but she dominated his life and thoughts as no one else ever had. He wanted to make tonight, their first night together, incredibly special for her so she might feel the same about him. He lowered his head and nipped her lower lip softly and then licked the hurt with his tongue. Her lips parted, inviting him in, and he deepened the kiss, lost in her unique taste. She tasted a little of chocolate and his own Cassie. His body responded instantly to her tantalizing taste, his cock getting harder and pressing against the zipper of his jeans. He trailed kisses from her lips across her jaw and down her neck to the hollow of her shoulder. Her skin was soft and silky. He breathed in her scent as he nipped and licked, hearing Cassie moan, and feeling her writhe underneath him. Each brush of her mound against him drove him crazy, and he had to rein in his instincts to strip her and take her quickly, marking her with his body and scent.

He lifted away and slid his hands under her shirt, running them up her ribcage, bringing the hem of the shirt up with them. Chase leaned in and lifted her slightly as Zach pulled the shirt up and over her head. Her eyes were half closed, and Chase leaned forward to take her lips in a passionate kiss. Zach took the opportunity while Cassie was distracted to strip her shorts and shoes from her, leaving her in nothing but her filmy bra and panties.

"Christ, Cassie. Are you trying to kill us?" Zach groaned as he took in her gorgeous body barely covered in the light-blue lace that just matched her eyes. He could clearly see the outline of her hard and tight nipples through her bra. His eyes wandered down to her barely-there thong panties where just a scrap of lace separated him from heaven.

* * * *

Nothing had ever felt this good. Chase's kisses and Zach's hands were so arousing, she thought she would burst into flames. Sex had never felt like this before. It was pleasant, but she had always wondered what the fuss was about. No man had ever taken this much time with her, seeing to her pleasure as Zach and Chase did. Her last boyfriend would kiss her a few times, tweak her nipples, then try and wedge inside her for a couple of minutes until he came. After he rolled over and fell asleep, she would lay wondering what was wrong with her, why she didn't react like women in the movies or in books. Now she knew there was nothing wrong with her.

The way Zach and Chase looked at her made her feel sexy, alive, and most of all, very wanted. They wanted her. She wanted to be enough for them. At this moment, they were everything to her, and she couldn't get enough of them touching and kissing her. For the first time in her life, she was greedy for pleasure.

She felt Chase flick the front closure of her bra, and with a little help from Zach, it slid down her arms and was tossed away. She closed her eyes as their hands caressed her breasts and softly flitted over her taut nipples. Their hands were rough from working outside, and she shivered as Zach began to kiss his way from her shoulders down to her nipples. Chase placed open-mouthed kisses on her thighs and stomach as Cassie went into sensory overload. A moan slipped from her lips. Zach and Chase kissed up and down her torso, and both settled their luscious mouths on her breasts. Zach nipped and licked at one nipple while Chase drew the other into his mouth hard, sucking while he flicked his tongue over the tip. She whimpered and moaned under their ministrations, her body writhing and twisting the covers on the bed. She felt Zach lift his head and kiss his way down her body and over her hip. Zach tugged her silky panties down her legs and tossed them away, quickly returning his lips to the swell of her stomach. He let his tongue slide from her hip down to the sensitive skin behind her knee. He kissed that knee then slid his tongue up her inner thigh just short of her pussy. She lifted her hips in frustration. He was driving her mad.

"Easy, Cassie. We'll get there. Just let Zach and I take care of you."

She heard Chase's soothing tone, and his hands held her down as he switched his attention to her other nipple while using his fingers on the abandoned one. Cassie felt a gush of moisture from her cunt and knew that Zach must see the honey coating her thighs. He leaned over and kissed her other hip, once again sliding his tongue down to the back of her knee, tickling the skin back there with his tongue and teeth. She knew what was coming next, and he didn't disappoint as he slid his tongue up her inner thigh oh-so-close to her wet slit. She couldn't keep still as his tongue tickled her inner thighs. She tried to close her legs against his inspection, but his broad shoulders kept her spread wide apart.

"Stay still, Cassie. You can't hide that pretty pussy from us." He ran his fingers through her drenched folds. She looked into Zach's eyes and saw lust and passion. He lifted his fingers to his mouth and licked her cream from his fingers.

"Damn, you taste good. I love how wet you are for us. Chase, you should get a taste of this, man."

Chase reached down with one hand and caressed her pussy, slowly running circles around her clit before pulling away, leaving her moaning in frustration. He licked at his fingers with relish.

"She does taste good. She smells wonderful, too. I can smell her arousal, and it's making my dick rock hard."

Her attention was torn from Chase as Zach parted her folds to expose her swollen clit. He leaned forward, and she could feel his hot breath against her pussy. He blew gently on her clit, and she felt it swell to attention and throb so hard, it was almost painful. Her breath caught at the first touch of his tongue on her pussy. He licked up and down her entire pussy and made circles around her clit but never quite touching it. She moaned and twisted in frustration, trying to get his tongue where she wanted it—on her clit. Chase continued to torment her nipples and smother her moans with his mouth and tongue.

"Please, Zach! Oh God, please make me come!" Her voice sounded strained and desperate.

"No, Cassie. You don't have permission to come yet. We will decide when you come." She could feel the vibration of Zach's voice against her oversensitive pussy, and it built her arousal even higher.

"Permission? What do you mean I don't have permission? I can come when I want!" She tried to sound mad, but it sounded breathless instead.

"No. You come only when we say you can. If you come without permission, we will punish you. Trust us. It will be worth it. Chase, come down here and help me out."

She felt Chase move on the bed and lean over the top of her pussy as Zach moved his tongue to her opening and began fucking her with it. Chase began to lick at her clit very lightly. It was just enough to keep her on the edge of release but not enough to send her over. Zach and Chase's strong hands kept her thighs spread wide, and she was helpless under their relentless mouths. Her head thrashed back and forth on the bed as they held her down, licking at her with their talented tongues. Her pleasure was so intense, it was almost painful, and she could feel her climax shimmering so close to her. Time seemed to stand still until she heard Zach's command.

"Come for us, Cassie. Come now."

Chase's mouth clamped over her clit and began to suck as he flicked the flat of his tongue back and forth. Her body went stiff, and the light behind her eyes seemed to turn white as pleasure like she had never known rushed through her body. She could feel it bloom from her pussy, spreading to her tight nipples and down to her toes, curling them in ecstasy. She screamed as the pleasure peaked in intensity, and her body shook as the spasms rolled through her like waves. Their mouths kept moving on her, less intense, but still sending smaller waves through her like aftershocks from an earthquake. She lost track of time as each delicious wave ran though her trembling body until, finally, she lay spent and exhausted. Before she could recover, Zach flipped her over on to her hands and knees, running kisses down her spine. She looked back to find her men peeling their clothes off.

She heard Zach ask Chase, "Mouth or pussy?"

Cassie looked at her men and couldn't help but admire their male beauty. They were all muscle without an ounce of fat anywhere. Wide shoulders and beautiful chests led down to tight, flat abs that she wanted to lick. Each man had just enough chest hair without being furry and a happy trail that led down to their very hard and large cocks. Zach and Chase stroked their cocks as they smiled down at her.

"I'll take that beautiful mouth first, bro."

"Then I get this wet pussy first. Open wide and suck Chase good, angel. Show us what you can do with that gorgeous mouth."

Chase climbed onto the bed and held his cock in front of her mouth. She had never enjoyed giving head before, but with them, she found she really wanted to. She was desperate to give them as much pleasure as they gave her. She opened and let her tongue run over the head, tasting the saltiness of his pre-cum. Her tongue swirled from base to tip.

"Don't tease, sweetheart. Suck me hard." Chase's hand tangled in her hair, pulling her gently where he wanted her. His cock slid over her tongue as she sucked on the crown, creating a tight seal. She began to move her head up and down on his cock, taking him a little deeper each time until he bumped the back of her throat, causing her to choke and cough a little.

"Easy, Cass. Don't try and take too much." Chase's hand wrapped around the base of his cock, making sure she didn't gag.

She heard the crinkle of a condom wrapper and then the brush of Zach's thighs against hers. He pushed her legs a little farther apart as one hand splayed across her stomach to pull her ass back and up toward him. His cock nudged at her pussy, pressing forward into her wet warmth. He pulled back, then pushed forward, pulled back, then pushed forward, a little farther each time. She felt her pussy walls stretch to accommodate his generous girth and each ridge of his cock as he pressed inside. Pleasure blossomed as she pushed back to meet each thrust, sucking up and down on Chase's cock as she moved. She had never felt so full of cock, her mouth and pussy overflowing with their hardness. Zach picked up pace and thrust into her harder and faster, and she lost Chase's cock from her mouth as she moaned from the pleasure.

Smack!

Zach smacked her ass cheek with his left hand while he fingered her clit with his right. Heat spread from where he had spanked her to her clit, the pain quickly turning to a burning pleasure.

"Keep sucking Chase, angel. Open now."

Chase fed his cock back into her mouth, and this time, he kept a hand at the back of her head to hold her there while his other hand kept her from choking.

"That's better. I want to see you suck him really hard. He loves that. Hollow out those cheeks, Cassie."

Cassie barely registered Zach's words as the ecstasy grew. She could feel Zach's cock hitting that sweet spot inside her with each thrust, and she knew she was building toward another climax.

Smack! Smack!

Her clit swelled from the spanking. Hazily, she realized that she was enjoying their punishment. It spiked her arousal even higher, even as it shocked her. She had never thought of herself as someone who enjoyed being dominated.

"Suck him hard, Cassie. Or I will move my fingers." Zach's fingers stilled on her clit, and she quickly tightened the seal around Chase's cock, hollowing out her cheeks, her tongue swirling with each pump of her mouth. She was desperate to come, and she moved so she was rubbing her clit against his fingers. He rubbed in quick circles around her clit in reward for her obedience.

"You better be close, Chase. She's so tight, I'm not going to be able to hold off much longer."

"I'm right with you, bro. Her mouth is amazing. Swallow me down, Cassie. Don't miss a drop."

Zach fucked her pussy harder and faster, and his fingers flew across her swollen clit. She felt Chase swell in her mouth and his hands tighten in her hair. His hot cum spilled over her tongue and down her throat. She swallowed it down as quickly as she could, trying not to lose a drop. He tasted salty and a little like the coffee that he liked to drink. It seemed he came forever and then he was done, moving in and out of her mouth so she could lick him clean.

"Good girl. Now come for Zach, sweetheart. Come hard for him."

Cassie teetered on the precipice of climax but allowed herself to fall over the edge with Chase's permission. Zach pinched her clit as he spanked her a few times, and she screamed their names as she came, and came hard. Colors and light blinded her for what felt like days but was really only seconds. Her arms gave out from under her, and she fell forward onto her shoulders. Zach tensed behind her and thrust into her hard and stayed there. She felt him pulse as his cum jetted into the condom, and his hands bit into her hips, holding her still. She heard his faint groan, and then he relaxed his body, leaning over and kissing her between her shoulder blades, drawing a shiver from her.

He gently pulled from her body as Chase pulled her into his arms, tucking her right next to him with her head under his chin. Zach returned from disposing of the condom and cuddled her back, kissed her neck, and stroked her hip and thigh in lazy circles.

Cassie felt her eyes start to droop, and she tried to fight but heard Chase say, "Sleep, sweetheart. We will wake you up soon and take you home. We know you have to work tomorrow."

She sighed and drifted off to sleep.

Chapter 8

The firehouse was lit up a few weeks later as Zach and Chase escorted Cassie, Jillian, and Rebecca to the monthly bingo night. All the fire trucks had been moved outside and tables and chairs had been moved into the large, open garage area. Cassie could see what looked like half the town milling around visiting with each other, passing the time, and reviewing the week that had passed.

"Becca, where do you want to sit?" Cassie glanced around, and luckily there were still some empty seats.

Cassie could see Jillian look around also, and Cassie could tell when she spotted Jackson Parks, Rebecca's younger brother and hunky firefighter extraordinaire. Jillian stiffened when she saw the handsome firefighter and pointed to a table far across the room.

"How about over there?"

Cassie was just about to agree when Jackson spotted the five of them, grinned, and waved them over to a table near the food setup. Chase and Zach grinned back at Jackson and started steering the women in that direction.

Zach smiled at Cassie and Jillian. "Y'all need to meet Jackson, Rebecca's brother. We all grew up together, and he's a great guy. I think you already met his brother, Ryan. He's the sheriff."

Cassie gave Jillian a pointed look. "Yes, we have met the sheriff but have only seen Jackson from a distance. We haven't met him yet."

Jackson grinned widely at the boys and his sister, and they all proceeded to male bond with some back slapping and good-natured ribbing. Jackson gave Rebecca a big hug and whispered something in her ear.

"Why don't you guys join me here at this table? Plenty of room. I'm helping with food tonight, so I need to be on this side of the room."

"You're not calling numbers tonight, Jack?"

"Nah, Zach. Sam is calling bingo tonight. Harry and I are doing the food with Becca's help, of course. We hope to get a good turnout as tonight's proceeds are earmarked to help fix the playground at the park. Equipment is really showing its age, and with the economy the way it is, there is no way any tax dollars are going to be available to replace it."

Chase smiled and nodded. "Well, count on Harper Construction when it's time to do the work. We would be happy to donate our time."

"Hell, yes," Zach agreed.

"We need to make introductions. Jackson, this is our girlfriend, Cassie, and her roommate, Jillian. Cassie, Jillian, this is Jackson Parks. And I assume you know your little sister, Rebecca."

Jackson smiled what appeared to be a million-dollar grin. "Pleased to meet you, ladies. Sure have heard a lot about you from Becca…and Ryan."

Jackson smiled at Cassie warmly, but his warm, hazel eyes drifted to Jillian and made a lazy perusal from toes to nose and back down again. From the heat in his eyes, he sure liked what he saw.

Cassie was sure that Jillian liked what she saw, too. Jackson was tall, probably a little over six feet, and well built. His firefighter-blue T-shirt with his company logo was stretched across broad shoulders that tapered down to flat abs that a male model would have been proud of. Cassie guessed that an impressive six pack was barely hidden beneath that shirt. His hair was blond like Rebecca's and a little shaggy, like he was overdue for a haircut. His skin was slightly tan from being outdoors a lot and covered a strong, square jaw that currently needed a shave. He was really a stunning man, Cassie thought. The third handsomest man in the room, after her two boys, of course.

Cassie smiled to herself. Jillian didn't stand a chance.

* * * *

They enjoyed the bingo, and at the halfway break, Cassie and Jillian excused themselves for a trip to the ladies' room while Rebecca went to help Jackson in the kitchen.

"Jackson seems really nice, Jillian. Not to mention gorgeous as hell."

Jillian's eyes narrowed as she looked at her best friend. "What are you trying to say, Cass?"

"Nothing, nothing. But, you could do worse. That's all I am saying."

"So you are saying something, then? Look, Cassie, we both know that I am not looking for any sort of relationship or anything. There is no point getting all hot and bothered over the sheriff and the hunky firefighter when nothing is ever going to happen."

"Jillian, what happened to your parents doesn't have to happen to you."

"No, but what chance does a slightly chubby redhead have in making two men happy? My mother was a freakin' goddess, and she couldn't keep one man happy. I am not going there, Cass. Drop it."

Cassie knew that look on Jillian's face. She wished she could take the hurt and pain from Jillian's childhood, but that wasn't going to be possible. Jillian was going to have to move past it.

"First of all, you are not chubby. You have fabulous curves that men love. Secondly, I think your father's infidelity had more to do with him than your mother. That's all I am saying."

Jillian tried to smile at Cassie. "You're my best friend in the whole fucking world, Cassie. But there is no way I will live the way my mother did. No fucking way."

Before Cassie could reply, another woman joined them in the

ladies' room and walked up to the mirror to check her makeup. Cassie couldn't help but notice that the woman was quite beautiful. She had dark hair cut in a stylish bob, and her face was perfectly made up from her icy, blue eyes to her generous, red mouth. Her purple silk dress with matching pumps seemed a little overkill for a bingo game. Cassie looked down at her own khaki shorts and blouse. Perhaps it was she who was underdressed?

The woman refreshed her lipstick and then turned toward them for a brief moment. Cassie started to smile at the woman and introduce herself. She didn't want to appear rude and knew that the town prided itself on being open and friendly at all times, even in a ladies' room.

The woman's eyes narrowed slightly as she glanced at Cassie and Jillian. Then she quickly dismissed them with a lift of her eyebrow and swept out of the restroom.

Jillian stared at Cassie with a shocked but amused look on her face. "Who the fuck was that?"

* * * *

Zach watched as Cassie and Jillian returned from the ladies' room. Cassie looked beautiful tonight in shorts that showed off her toned, tan legs and a red blouse that just hinted at the cleavage that Zach had already become quite fond of. Her long, blonde hair was loose around her shoulders, and her eyes were sparkling as she looked back at him. He couldn't believe how lucky he and Chase were. Cassie was the fulfillment of all their hopes and dreams, and she was theirs. The ache in his soul was gone. She had replaced it with her warmth and passion. He could only hope he healed her, too.

He threw his arm around her shoulders as Chase put his arm around her waist. They couldn't seem to get enough of being close to her.

"Well, now that's someone I didn't expect to see tonight."

Zach turned at Jackson's words and stared at the woman he had hoped to never see again.

Fuck. Shit. Amelia.

Zach looked at Chase, and Chase seemed to be as shocked as he was. The last time they had seen Amelia was five years ago. Zach had been home between tours in Afghanistan, and Amelia had told him and Chase that she was going to marry some attorney in Dallas. She wanted more from life than he and Chase could give her. She needed a man to take care of her, and the two of them hadn't been doing the job. She had been brutally honest with them. She loved fucking them, but she needed more than a good lay.

As he stared at her, he wondered what he and Chase had ever seen in her in the first place. She had always been beautiful, and he hated to think that he and Chase had been so shallow that looks were all that mattered. Amelia had never been warm, loving, and full of laughter like Cassie. Amelia had been, well, fun to fuck. She had an insatiable sexual appetite. He and Chase had been mesmerized by her sexual power, but the appeal had quickly faded. The fact was Amelia was difficult to be around and incredibly spoiled. She had sulked and pouted through most of their relationship to get whatever she wanted. Zach wondered if anything had changed. The years appeared to have hardened her a little, and she seemed cold and aloof despite the wide smile she gave them as she crossed the room toward them.

"Zach! Chase! Darlings!"

Zach watched as Amelia made a beeline for them and proceeded to throw her arms around each of them and give them a wet, hard kiss, edging Cassie out of their arms.

"Darlings! I was hoping to see you tonight. Are you surprised to see me?"

Amelia rubbed Zach's chest with her open palm, giving him a smile he remembered. The smile that said, "I want you to fuck me and fuck me hard." Zach cleared his throat and removed Amelia's hand from his chest. *Not in this fucking lifetime.* Zach looked at Chase and saw that his eyes held the same disgust.

"Amelia, how nice to see you. Yes, we are definitely surprised. I want you to meet our girlfriend, Cassie Ames. Cassie, this is Amelia Winters Thompson. She used to live in Plenty several years ago." Zach drew Cassie into his arms, and Chase moved to the other side of Cassie. Zach wanted to make sure Amelia got the picture really clear. They were with Cassie now, and neither of them would do anything to endanger that relationship. Cassie was the future. Amelia was the past and the distant past at that. He could only hope that Amelia wasn't up to her old tricks. The self-absorbed she-devil could simply not be trusted.

* * * *

Cassie looked at the woman whom she had seen in the restroom and had been dismissed summarily by. Amelia wasn't looking at her any friendlier now. In fact, she was looking at Cassie as if she were a piece of lint. Something to be flicked away and never thought about again. Too bad Cassie wasn't going anywhere. Cassie remembered what Rebecca had told her about Amelia, and she wasn't going to let this nasty woman get the best of her.

"It's so nice to meet you, Amelia. Are you here for a visit?" Cassie slid her arms around both her boys and smiled up at them. *Take that, bitch.*

Amelia gave her a cold smile that didn't reach her eyes. "Not a visit. I am planning to move back to Plenty. There are just some things you can't get in the big city." Amelia gave a look to Cassie, leaving her in no doubt what those things she couldn't get were— Zach and Chase. "I am sure Zach and Chase told you all about how we dated several years ago. My, what fun we had, didn't we, darlings? These two were pretty wild in their younger days."

"No, I am afraid they never mentioned you. How many years ago did you say it was?" Cassie arched her eyebrows at Amelia and ran her hand up and down Zach's back. She could feel the way he had stiffened since Amelia had come into the room. Cassie guessed that Zach didn't remember all that fun as clearly as Amelia did.

Zach answered for Amelia. "It was a lifetime ago, Cassie. Ancient history. I am too busy thinking about our future to think about the past." And then Zach gave that killer smile with those God-given dimples. Chase leaned over and kissed the back of Cassie's neck and grinned.

"Damn straight, sweetheart. I can only think about our future."

Cassie smiled gratefully at her men. She got their message, and she appreciated that they weren't afraid to make it clear in front of Amelia and their friends. They were good men.

"Well, it was lovely to see you, darlings. Let's get together soon and catch up and talk about old times." Amelia leaned forward and ran her hand along Chase's shoulder suggestively before turning and walking back to a group of people near the door.

Jillian, as usual, was the first to speak and break the tension. "Wow! That woman is just exhausting to be around and, might I say, downright unpleasant!"

Cassie couldn't help but erupt in laughter. Jillian always managed to size up a person for who they were right away. She really had a gift.

Jackson laughed, too. "Yep, that's Amelia—exhausting and unpleasant. That pretty much sums her up. Although, you could add cold, calculating, spoiled, and well, maybe Zach and Chase would like to add an adjective or two."

"I could add a few adjectives."

Cassie turned in surprise as an attractive, dark-haired woman walked up and gave Zach and Chase big hugs.

Jackson laughed. "I'm sure you could, Mrs. Harper."

Zach and Chase's mother.

She could see the family resemblance, although, Chase seemed to favor her the most.

"Hey, Mom. We didn't see you earlier. Where are Dad and

Pops?" Zach kissed his mother's cheek.

"In the buffet line, of course. We just got here. Peter had business in Tampa, so that's where we spent the day."

Chase leaned down and kissed his mother. "Glad you made it tonight. We want to introduce you to Cassie. Mom, this is Cassie Ames. Cassie, this is our mother, Nancy Harper."

Nancy Harper's eyes were the soft-blue of Zach's. She gave Cassie a big smile that lit up her already beautiful face.

"I'm so glad to meet you! These boys have been going on and on about you. Cassie this, and Cassie that. I hope they are being good boys and treating you right. If not, you just let me know."

Zach and Chase groaned.

"It's nice to meet you, Mrs. Harper. They are treating me just fine. You obviously raised them right."

Nancy beamed at the praise before turning to Jackson. "Now, Jackson, aren't you going to introduce me to your new girlfriend. She's a pretty one."

Jillian's face turned a fiery red.

"Of course I will, Mrs. Harper. This is Cassie's best friend, Jillian Miller." Jackson had a smug look on his face.

Jillian offered her hand. "I'm afraid there's been a little misunderstanding. I'm not Jackson's girlfriend. But it is very nice to meet you, ma'am."

Nancy looked thoughtful as she shook hands with Jillian. "Are you sure, dear? Not that it's any of my business, of course. Chase, were you talking to Amelia? That woman is trouble."

Chase shook his head. "Hell no. I wouldn't waste my breath on her. She came up to us. I think I speak for my brother when I say that I am none too proud of ever having had a relationship with her."

"Amen, bro."

"Well, listen to your mother when I tell you to stay far away from her. I heard she is getting a divorce from that poor husband of hers. I'm guessing she's here to troll for a new one, or two, in your case. It will be over my dead body that she marries you two."

* * * *

Chase looked closely at Cassie to gauge her feelings about the encounter. Was she upset? He and Zach hadn't kept their relationship with Amelia a secret on purpose. They just honestly didn't think about her anymore. She had been a mistake they had made many years ago, a mistake that they didn't intend to repeat, no matter how much Amelia rubbed against them and gave them fuck-me looks. Amelia seemed so cold compared to Cassie that they would have to be crazy to ever get involved with her again. And he and Zach were not crazy.

He hadn't seen Zach this content since before he went to the Middle East. Cassie's gentle presence seemed to soothe Zach in a way that no one had been able to. Chase wanted to heal Cassie in return. She had demons from her past, and he was more than ready to chase them away. First, he needed to make sure Amelia hadn't chased her away. He needed to get her home and away from the poison effect of Amelia.

He remembered his mama saying that it was never a good idea to piss off a woman, whether it was intentional or not. His dads used to pretty much say the same thing. "Just apologize, son, whether you are wrong or not. Being together is more important than who was right or who was wrong. Your pride will be cold comfort when you are sleeping on the couch."

And damned if Chase wanted to sleep on the couch with Zach.

* * * *

The ride home in the truck was quiet. Finally, Cassie decided to break the silence. "Did you love her? It's okay if you did. It was a long time ago, after all."

Zach looked sideways at Chase. Chase was the first to answer.

"No, and hell no, sweetheart. We were not in love with Amelia. We will admit to being in lust with Amelia. But love, no. She used us, and we were young and dumb and let her. I don't even want to compare what we feel for you in the same breath. It doesn't do our feelings justice. We didn't feel a fraction for her that we do for you. Please don't give her another thought."

Chase's eyes pleaded with her to see his sincerity. "For real? She's very beautiful. Sometimes I wonder if I can make two men happy." She took a deep breath, and her blue eyes went round as they darted back and forth between the two most gorgeous men she had ever laid eyes on.

"Hell yes, you make us happy. We've never been happier." This time is was Zach who answered. He looked at her with his heart in his intense, blue eyes. "We adore you, and we would do anything for you. We know it is fast. But we want you to know how we feel, Cassie." Zach pulled into the drive, put the truck in park, and moved closer.

"Well, gosh, boys, I feel the same way. I've just been worried about a relationship with two men. How can one woman satisfy two men?"

Zach gave her a slow grin. "I don't know about Chase, but I feel mighty satisfied. What about you, Chase?"

"Hell, yes, I'm satisfied. I've never been this satisfied. This girl's downright wearing me out, in fact."

Cassie launched herself at Zach and then Chase. She hadn't been this happy in, well, maybe forever. She was finally putting the past behind her.

Chase hugged her from behind, kissing that sensitive spot on her neck that made her eyes roll back in her head.

"Whatdya say, Zach? We take this girl inside and show her how we feel?"

"Good idea, Chase. She has been such a good girl tonight. Perhaps we need to reward her."

Cassie couldn't help but shiver at the thought of what her reward might be.

Chapter 9

Cassie snuggled closer to Zach as he carried her through the house and out the patio doors. He was always carrying her somewhere. "Where are we going? I thought I was going to get a reward."

Cassie pouted a little as she gazed into Zach's handsome face. She leaned up and traced a dimple with her tongue feeling him shudder a little and smiled. Being with her boys always made her feel sexy and powerful. She loved how they responded to her touch as much as she loved how she responded to them.

"You are getting a reward. You'll love this."

Zach set her feet down by the hot tub that could probably seat six comfortably. Steam rose from the surface of the swirling water, and it overflowed into the swimming pool in a sparkling waterfall effect.

"Strip."

Cassie's eyes flew to Zach's. "What did you say?"

"I said strip, angel. Your reward can't start until you are buck naked. So get out of those clothes. Now." Cassie heard the steel in Zach's voice, and as always, her body responded to it by gushing honey from her pussy.

Traitor, she thought.

Her body was a traitor, but she couldn't deny that she loved it. His dominance never ceased to arouse her, and she knew that he would never hurt her. He used it to bring her pleasure only. Zach demanded her arousal, and damned if she could stop herself. She had put up a token resistance to playing the submissive, but her body had overruled her at every turn.

Chase, on the other hand, only played at dominating her. He liked to tease and seduce her responses, playing with her body until she begged him to finish her.

She unbuttoned her blouse and handed it to Zach. Her shorts and socks were next along with her shoes. She stood before him in her red, satin bra and panty set. Since she had started dating them, she had replaced all her underthings with items designed to inflame their desire. She needn't have bothered. Her boys were hard and ready at all times.

Chase strolled onto the patio carrying a stack of towels and what looked like a small gym bag. He dropped the stack and looked her up and down with lust in his eyes.

"Nice, very nice. Sexy undies always make me hard as a fuckin' rock, Cassie."

Zach growled. "She isn't supposed to be wearing anything at all. Strip, now."

Cassie laughed and scrambled out of her bra and panties, handing them over to Zach, who then handed all her clothes to Chase. "Take these inside. She doesn't get them back until she earns them back."

Chase laughed as he went back inside the house. "You are such a hard-ass, bro."

Zach crossed his arms and scowled. "I want this to be a reward tonight. So you need to trust us, and do as we ask. Do you trust us?"

Cassie nodded and ran her hands around his waist to bring him in for a hug. "Yes, I do. I have never trusted any man the way I do you and Chase. But you know that I am still getting used to this submissive stuff. I am still not sure how I feel about it, honestly. I know that my body loves it, but my mind is still trying to come to terms with it."

Zach's face softened. "I understand. You know, we would never hurt you. I'm a dominating son of a bitch, but I adore you. When you let me take control, it turns me on like nothing else, fills me up like nothing else. Give up a little control tonight, Cassie. I promise you won't regret it. Maybe your body can help your mind be okay with this. We care about you and respect you, I swear."

Cassie smiled up at Zach. "I am all yours tonight. I can't wait for my reward. Let's convince my mind."

She watched as Zach reached down into the pile of towels and picked up a black piece of cloth.

"Turn around, and close your eyes."

Cassie took a big breath as Zach waited for her compliance. She really did trust them, she realized with wonder.

This trust feels so freeing. I can just sit back and let them take control. What a luxury.

"Anytime you want to stop, Cassie, just say the word 'red.' Everything will stop if you say that."

Cassie slowly turned around, facing away from Zach, and closed her eyes. Zach wrapped the cloth around her eyes tightly, and she heard the Velcro fastening stick. He gave it a tug to assure himself it wasn't going anywhere.

She felt herself being turned back toward him. The cloth actually had padding over the eye area, and she realized that it blocked out all light. She couldn't see a thing, and that fact seemed to heighten her other senses. She could smell the chlorine from the swimming pool and hot tub, Zach's spicy male scent, and her own arousal.

His rough fingertips brushed over her nipples, making them tighten painfully. His fingers trailed down the swell of her stomach, between her legs, to her already wet pussy. He let his fingers glide in her pussy, and his thumb swirled around her clit, drawing a moan from her. She heard him chuckle.

"I think you like giving up control, Cassie."

She opened her mouth to reply, but his mouth came down on hers possessively, demanding a response from her. His tongue rubbed along hers and explored every inch of her mouth as if he owned it. By the time he lifted his head, she was breathless, and her knees were weak. She didn't think she could hold herself up, but it wasn't a problem as he handed her to another set of strong arms. Chase. She would know his scent anywhere. He and Zach smelled similar, but Chase had a woodier, citrus smell that weakened her knees even further.

His mouth came down, but instead of dominating her, he nipped and licked at her lips until she groaned with frustration, trying to move her mouth over his and suck in his tongue. He continued nipping and licking across her jaw until he got to her ear. His tongue followed the shell of her ear and then he unexpectedly bit down on her earlobe. Not hard enough to draw blood, but hard enough that her clit throbbed in response. She threw her head back and moaned as her arousal hitched up several notches. She rubbed her body against Chase's, trying to get some friction on her slit. She felt him push her gently away.

"Not yet. Trust us, when you come tonight, it will be harder than you have ever come before."

That's pretty hard. I've never come like this in my life the way I do with them.

She heard a zipper, two sets of warm hands tweaking her nipples, then a cold piece of metal on them. The metal tightened until she gasped. At her gasp, they slightly lessened the pinch, but it was still uncomfortable. They each gave a clip a tug that went straight to her clit. The pain quickly morphed into a pleasurable ache that made her pussy clench with the need to be filled.

"Very pretty. Every time you move, it will feel like a pinch from our fingers."

One of them reached down between her legs and ran a finger along her drenched folds. She was pulled toward the hot tub, and strong arms helped lower her into the swirling water. The water immediately relaxed her, and she leaned back on the seat as their hands ran over her sensitized skin, drawing a moan from her. They were right. Every time she moved, the clamps pulled and tugged on her sensitive nipples, sending sparks of pleasure through her body.

She felt strong hands begin to massage her back and shoulders while another set of hands began massaging her feet. They worked the muscles firmly, but gently, until she was as limp as a noodle. Every now and then, one of them would tug on a nipple clamp, sending more moisture to her aching pussy. It felt so empty, and she needed it filled soon. Only their hard cocks would fill it for her. The pleasure they could give never ceased to amaze her.

* * * *

Cassie lay back in the cradle of his hips. Her lips parted as she moaned every so often when they hit a sensitive spot. Chase worked his hands down her arms and massaged her hands and wrists, then back up to each side of her head where he ran his hands through her hair and began rubbing circles on her forehead above her blindfold.

Zach was working on her feet and ankles, making her squirm on Chase's very hard cock. Zach gently dropped Cassie's foot in the water and gave him a look. Chase lifted Cassie from his chest so she sat straighter in the water. He held her and rubbed her shoulders as his brother brushed his cock against her lips, demanding entry.

Cassie's mouth opened, and his brother fed her inch after inch of his cock. Watching her suck his brother made his own cock swell harder against her ass, and he gritted his teeth as he shifted her to sit on the seat. Cassie moved her head up and down on Zach's cock, taking it a little farther into her mouth each time.

Her fingers came up and played with Zach's balls, rolling them gently with her fingers and scraping her nails across the sensitive flesh. Zach's eyes were closed, and Chase knew from experience that he wouldn't last long with Cassie's talented mouth working on him. Chase tugged at the clamps on her nipples, and she seemed to suck Zach harder and faster. He saw Zach signal him to do it again. He gave them another few tugs, one at a time, and then together. Cassie moaned and redoubled her efforts to get Zach off, saliva running down her chin and glistening on Zach's hard shaft.

Chase reached around and rubbed circles around her clit, not touching it directly, but giving the sides light tickles. She wiggled her ass, trying to get his fingers where she wanted them, but he quickly moved them and gave the clamps another tug. Zach was gritting his teeth to hold back and pulled out of Cassie's mouth with a pop. Cassie cried out a little, trying to pull him back, but Chase turned her for a quick kiss.

"Not yet, sweetheart. We have more in store for you. Come up to the side of the hot tub and lean over the edge. I put a towel there to cushion you."

Chase helped Cassie get into position with her ass in the air and her torso lying on the deck. Zach was pouring lube all over a small plug and gave Chase a grin.

"Want to do the honors, bro?"

Chase took the plug from Zach and began massaging the globes of her ass. Zach spread her cheeks apart, revealing her tight, little rosette. He leaned forward and ran his tongue along her seam and around her rear hole. Cassie jerked and froze.

"What—what are you doing?"

Her voice sounded panicked, and Chase wanted her to relax. This wouldn't be possible if she was tensed up. "Relax, baby, and let Zach work his tongue on you. We have to stretch you if we want to be able to take you together. We promised you pleasure, right? Just trust us." He ran his hand comfortingly along her spine while Zach continued to work his tongue in her back door.

"Oh, oh, oh, it feels, oh, God!" Cassie writhed under Zach's tongue, but they held her down easily.

Zach reached behind him for the bottle of lube. Chase knew his brother would be generous with it as a virgin ass needed to be stretched slowly and carefully. They both wanted Cassie to enjoy this. Zach squeezed the lube down her crack and used his middle finger to work it into her ass. Cassie moaned and bucked but didn't protest as Zach worked his finger all the way in and began to fuck her with it in and out.

* * * *

Cassie moaned as her backside was stretched by Zach's thick digit. It wasn't as painful as she thought it might be. There was the stretching and then a burn, just before her ring of muscles gave way. His finger had slid in to the hilt, and as he finger-fucked her, he rubbed nerves she never knew existed. It felt dark and naughty, but so good, she couldn't tell him to stop. She didn't hold back her groan of pleasure as Zach's fingers slipped out and caressed her dark hole.

"Good girl, Cassie. We knew you would like this. Let's give you something more."

She felt an object being pressed against her opening.

Zach petted her back and crooned soothing words. "Push back against the plug, sweetheart. We have to stretch you if you are ever going to be able to take both of us. That's it, push."

Cassie pushed back, but the plug felt much larger than Zach's finger. She felt the stretch and the burn again as the plug seemed to flare out wider than she thought she would ever be able to take. Just when she thought she should stop them, hands tugged on the clamps and her bottom opened, letting the plug slide in. It fit snugly in her backside, and she felt someone wiggle it, sending frissons of pleasure to her clit. Cassie instinctively turned to look at the plug but could only see darkness as the blindfold stole her sight. She felt Zach's gentle hands turn her face and something softly brush her lips. She could tell his cock was directly in front of her face.

"I get the hint, Zach." Cassie laughed and let her tongue trace the vein that she knew ran on the underside of his length. His cock jerked in reaction, and she heard his sharp intake of breath at her touch, her senses heightened by her blindness.

She ran her hands up and down his velvety length, loving how hard he felt in her hands. She opened wide to take as much of him as she could, swirling her tongue back and forth as she moved up and down his steely shaft. Chase began to fuck the plug in and out, and the sensitive nerves sent shivers up her spine. She moaned around Zach's cock, sucking harder and taking him deeper until he was nudging the back of her throat. She quickly got into a rhythm and could tell from the groans and pants from Zach that he was enjoying the attention. He thrust gently into her mouth, his balls drawn up tight in pleasure.

"Ah fuck, angel. That feels so fucking good. Faster, baby! I'm gonna come—fuck!"

Zach thrust once more in to her mouth and held himself there. She could feel him jerking in her mouth, spurting his hot seed across her tongue and down her throat as quickly as she could swallow it. His taste was slightly different than Chase's—spicier—and she drank every drop greedily. When Zach was done, he pulled slowly, almost regretfully, from her mouth.

"Christ, Cass. That mouth should be illegal in all fifty states."

Cassie grinned and felt her body warm with the praise. She had been worried about pleasing two men, but they certainly seemed happy enough.

"My turn."

Before Cassie could do anything, Chase spread her legs wide and thrust himself into her dripping pussy from behind all the way to the hilt.

"Chase!" Cassie rocked forward on the edge of the hot tub, splashing everywhere from the power of the thrust. The clamps pulled sharply on her nipples, sending lightning to her already swollen clit.

"Take it easy on her, Chase. Don't break her for chrissake. She has to last us a lifetime," Zach said snarkily.

Chase froze. "Sorry, sweetheart. I guess I was a little anxious. Are you okay?" She could hear the sheepishness in his voice.

"Only if you don't start moving your ass, Chase. Fuck me!"

With the plug in her ass, Chase felt even larger than normal in her swollen cunt. He moved her slightly to the right so a jet of water was pointed directly at her clit.

"This is your reward. We want you to come as many times as you can," Chase whispered in her ear.

The stream of water tickled and massaged her clit, and she was on the edge of climax almost immediately. She groaned as he began to fuck her slowly and play with the plug at the same time. Her first orgasm came hard and fast. She squeezed her eyes shut and curled her toes as the climax zipped through her small frame.

She barely had a chance to catch her breath before she could feel the build toward release again as each stroke rubbed the sweet spot inside her and the plug in her ass stimulated a completely different set of pleasure receptors. Her brain started to short-circuit with the double sensation. Zach reached forward and tugged on the nipple clamps, sending lightning bolts of pleasure to her already aching and sensitive clit. The pulsing jet of water caressed her pussy. She pushed back against Chase as he began to speed up his thrusts, slamming into her harder and harder. A fine sheen of sweat formed on her skin, and her breathing was ragged.

She heard Zach's soft voice urging her on. "Come on, angel. Come for us. We want another one. Let go."

Chase's cock continued to piston in an out of her, and Zach tugged on the clamps. She shot off like a rocket. Stars and white light as her body tensed, and the rolling waves of pleasure ran through her, sending tremors all the way to her fingertips. She moaned their names as she felt her pussy squeezing Chase's cock, and Zach released one clamp and then the other. The edge of pain as the blood rushed into her nipples set off another set of waves through her cunt, all the way up her back and down her legs, and settled in her clit. She felt Chase thrust hard and then stiffen as his cock seemed to swell even larger, pressing against the plug. The pleasure was almost painful in its intensity as he poured his cum into her sensitive pussy. He groaned and then slumped on her back, pulling her face back for a tender kiss and removing the blindfold. She blinked as her eyes adjusted to the lighting on the patio.

She felt Chase's chuckle against her back. "You are going to be the death of us, Cassie. We're dead men walkin'."

Zach smirked as he helped her out from under Chase and out of the pool. "But what a way to go, bro. With a big fuckin' grin on my face."

Chase quickly and discreetly disposed of the condom while Zach wrapped a fluffy, white towel around her and lifted her into his arms. Zach strode toward the bedroom with a backward glance at Chase.

"Round two in the bedroom. Last one there, comes last, too!"

Chapter 10

Zach looked out the kitchen window to the front driveway. Cassie was due in a few minutes, and he was anxious for her arrival. Things with Cassie just kept getting better and better, and it wasn't just the sex. He couldn't remember being this happy. Ever.

Cassie's warmth and passion were all he could want in a woman. He and Chase had never thought they could find a single woman that responded to his dominant nature and Chase's playful one. And unlike Amelia, she didn't demand they buy her presents. In fact, she didn't demand anything but their respect. It was strange being in a relationship that wasn't full of drama, but they liked it.

They simply needed to convince her that they were the men to make her happy. He had spent four years doing covert missions in war zones. Convincing one tiny, little woman that they were fucking Prince Charmings shouldn't be a problem.

An engine growled, and a cloud of dust billowed behind a silver Lexus going way too fast down their long driveway. Zach sighed and closed his eyes in frustration.

Amelia.

It seemed everywhere he or Chase went these last few weeks, Amelia was somehow there. They had seen her in the diner, the pizza parlor, and the hardware store. Zach didn't think that Amelia knew that Plenty had a hardware store, let alone shopped in it.

Cassie had noticed, but had kept silent on the subject. A small part of him was afraid that Cassie didn't care. Perhaps she was tired of them already? Maybe she wanted out? The thought made his stomach tighten and his heart hurt.

Amelia's car turned and headed for the barn where Chase was feeding the horses. He needed to get rid of her. Now. He didn't want her here when Cassie showed up. This shit needed to stop. What was wrong with this woman that she couldn't take a fucking hint?

* * * *

Chase petted the nose of Cyrano, his favorite horse. He had finished feeding the horses in record time. Cassie would be here soon, and she had promised to make spaghetti for dinner. She was a pretty good cook, although she kept saying that Jillian was better.

He seemed to have a smile on his face all the time these days. Everyone thought he was happy all the time, but he knew that this happiness was different. It was bone deep and profound. He was on the verge of having the life he had always dreamed about.

Chase had never cared that he had stayed in Plenty while Zach went overseas. Zach didn't believe that, but it was the truth. Chase loved music. He loved his family and the town more. Besides, he didn't have the killer instinct that it took to make it in the music industry. That wasn't the kind of life he wanted to live.

A silver Lexus whipped past the door of the barn and came to a screeching halt, kicking up dust ten feet in the air. Chase's jaw clenched in anger. *Speaking of someone with killer instinct...*

Amelia exited gracefully and walked toward him on high heels, their sharp points sinking into the ground with each step. She was crazy wearing those shoes out here. But then Amelia was crazy. Devious too. Amelia was also beautiful, of course, in a cold, icy way. Despite the heat of October, she wore an off-white trench coat belted at the waist. Her long fingernails resembled talons with their blood-red nail polish. He once again wondered what he had ever seen in her.

"Chase, darling! I'm so glad I caught you out here!"

Chase did not have time for this shit.

"What do you want, Amelia. I'm busy."

Amelia ran her finger up his arm and pouted her full, red lips. "Is that anyway to talk to a friend, Chase? We used to be such good friends, too."

Chase pulled her hand off his arm. "We used to be a lot of things. We aren't anymore. What the hell do you want anyway?"

"That's a good question. I want to know that, too."

Chase looked up as Zach strode into the room looking pissed the fuck off. Usually, it was him that had the hair trigger temper. Not this time. Zach looked ready to throw Amelia's ass off their property.

"Zach, darling, you really need to calm down. I have a perfectly legitimate reason for being here. I want to buy a horse."

Zach quirked an eyebrow in surprise.

"Since when do you ride, Amelia? I believe you called them smelly beasts at one time. You need to leave, and don't come back. We don't have anything for you."

Amelia's throaty laugh echoed through the large barn. Chase knew she was up to no good. He knew that look.

"But you do have something I want, darling, and I have something I know you've missed."

Chase and Zach watched in shock as Amelia loosened the belt on her coat and let it drop to the barn floor. She stood there completely naked except for her fuck-me heels. Chase could see Zach's face tighten in anger.

"Get your fucking clothes on, Amelia, and get your ass off this property. Now." Zach used his most commanding voice. He was barely holding himself in check, Chase could tell.

"Yes, you should definitely get your clothes on, and get your skanky butt out of here before I go all Chicago on your ass!"

Chase closed his eyes in horror. Cassie was here, and she was pissed. Cassie stomped into the barn and got right up in Amelia's face. *Oh shit.*

* * * *

Cassie could feel the anger coursing through her as she eyed the naked woman trying to steal her men. She had fucking had it with this bitch. So much for turning the other cheek and letting the boys handle this. Apparently, the little princess didn't take hints well. Cassie needed to step in and make a few things clear.

Amelia just looked at her with amusement. "My, my, so angry. Looks like Tinkerbell is a little jealous. Can't keep your men happy, sweetie? Perhaps you should let me take over."

Cassie saw red. The witch had hit her where she was weakest. She was still insecure about satisfying two men. Especially when those men were as virile and handsome as Chase and Zach.

"Tinkerbell? This Tinkerbell is going to throw your ass out of this barn!" Cassie reached down and picked up the coat and tossed it at Amelia.

"Cover up, and get the hell out."

Amelia just smirked. "I don't hear Chase and Zach telling me to leave. I think they want me to stay."

Before Cassie could reply, a red-faced Zach stepped between them.

"Stay out of this, Cassie. Chase and I can handle this."

Cassie took a challenging stance. "Really? So far I haven't seen you handle anything. You act like her feelings are more important than mine. Are they?"

Chase grabbed her arm and spun her around to look at him. He looked pissed as hell. "Do you really believe that? You are the most important thing to Zach and me. You're our whole fucking world."

Cassie tried to harden her heart at Chase's sweet words.

"All I know, Chase, is what I see. And what I see is you two walking on eggshells when it comes to Amelia. I've been waiting for you to do something, but so far, nothing."

Zach's hard voice broke through her haze of anger.

"Then see this, Cassie."

Cassie gaped in shock as Zach grabbed Amelia's arm and led her firmly out of the barn and toward her car. He opened the car door and practically lifted her and placed her in the seat, slamming the car door shut. Amelia started the car and slammed it into reverse, peeling backwards and almost hitting a tree. She righted the car and sped down the driveway toward the main road, a cloud of dust following her.

Zach strode back into the barn, his face a determined mask.

Oh fuck. He does not look happy.

Cassie took a few steps back only to run into Chase. Zach crowded her front, and she could see his jaw working in anger. "Uh, guys, maybe we should go into the house and—"

Zach's kiss took possession of her lips. It was an angry kiss, but Cassie could not help responding to his hunger. When he drew back, she was dizzy with need and want. Her pussy creamed in response to his dominance.

* * * *

Zach took a deep breath to control his anger and frustration. Had Cassie actually thought they gave a rat's furry ass about Amelia? He had simply tried to ignore the woman so it wouldn't get ugly. Well, it had, and now he and Chase needed to make sure that Cassie knew what she meant to them. She meant everything.

He bent over and pressed his shoulder into her middle, lifting her in a fireman hold. He heard her squeal in protest but just looked back and motioned to Chase. She wriggled trying to get free, but he just wrapped an arm around her legs and carried her over to the stacked bales of hay. He dumped her on a bale and began tugging her shoes off. The horses could watch if they wanted to. He had to have her now.

Chase joined in, and they had her naked in seconds. He scowled at the hay bale. He didn't want it to scratch her delicate skin. Chase came to the rescue and threw a horse blanket over the hay bale. Zach laid Cassie on top of the blanket, her legs off the edge.

"Grab her arms, Chase, and hold her down. I don't want her squirming around."

Chase chuckled and grabbed Cassie's wrists and anchored them over her head. So far, Cassie had allowed them to do as they pleased. He didn't want to force her. He shouldered between her legs so they were spread wide. Her pussy was pink and wet, begging for his touch. He drew a finger slowly around her swollen clit. Cassie moaned at the contact.

"You're very wet, angel. Do you want us? Do you want this? Never doubt how much we want you. I think about this pussy all fucking day long."

He swiped his tongue once over her clit, and she cried out in response.

"Answer me, angel. Do you want us?" He leaned forward and gave her clit another lick. Cassie groaned in frustration.

"I'd answer him if I were you," Chase teased, "he's not going to let you come until you do. By the way, you're my world, too. Amelia doesn't mean anything to me. There's only you."

Cassie opened her beautiful, blue eyes and bit her bottom lip, swollen from his kiss. "Yes, I want you both. I've been afraid. I've been afraid that I wasn't enough to make you happy."

Chase rolled his eyes and sighed. "Do we look unhappy? I've never been happier. I know that Zach has never been happier. We fucking love you, Cassie. I've never said that to a woman before."

Cassie's eyes were bright with unshed tears. "You love me? Really? I love you, too! Both of you!" Cassie tried to sit up, but Chase held her down easily.

Zach felt his heart open. This woman had healed his soul. He didn't realize how much pain he had held onto until it was gone. He had to say the words. "I love you, too, Cassie. You've made me feel whole again. I haven't felt that in a long time.

Tears did fall from her eyes now. "You make me whole, too. I've never felt so safe and loved in my life. I feel I finally have the family that I've always dreamed of. I love both of you so much. Charlie was right."

Chase chuckled. "What was Charlie right about, sweetheart?" He began to kiss her neck and shoulders while his left hand still held her wrists over her head.

Cassie giggled and smiled. Zach wanted to make her smile like that every day for the rest of her life.

"She said that with two men there was more love. She was right."

* * * *

Cassie's heart ached with love for her men. She put the last of her insecurities away. She didn't need them anymore.

Zach began tracing around her clit with his finger sending tingles shooting through her abdomen. Her pussy was already wet and swollen. She knew he could see honey dripping from her cunt. She needed to come badly.

"Please, Zach, please let me come."

She knew she was in trouble when Zach simply continued circling her clit. It was driving her crazy. She tried to move, but Chase held her down easily.

"Chase! Make him let me come!" She appealed.

Chase had the audacity to smirk. He began pinching her nipples with his other hand, making her twist and writhe.

Zach slid two fingers inside and began slowly fucking her in and out, pushing her closer to release. "If you want to come, Cassie, all you have to do is ask for what you want. What do you want?"

Cassie whimpered. "I want you to make me come."

Zach shook his head. "Not good enough."

Chase closed his lips over a nipple and sucked, his tongue flicked the hard bud. Cassie shook with the need to climax.

"Tell me exactly what you want, and you will get it."

Cassie couldn't take anymore. She desperately needed to come.

"Please, Zach! Lick and suck my clit! Make me come!"

Zach took mercy on her and obeyed her immediately. His fingers kept up the fucking rhythm while his mouth closed over her clit. He licked and sucked her clit. Her orgasm hit her hard. Her body bowed and her legs shook. Spirals of pleasure ran through her until she lay limp and spent.

She hazily watched Zach dig something from his pocket. A condom. He opened his pants and slipped it on his hard cock. He leaned over and took a nipple in his mouth and nipped at it with his teeth. Chase sucked at the other nipple until she was begging to be fucked. She needed to be filled with their hard cocks.

Zach lined up and entered her with one hard stroke. Chase played with her nipples and kissed her shoulders. Zach began fucking her slowly at first, then faster. He thrust in and out of her, his balls slapping her ass with each stroke. Each stroke rubbed her clit, starting her climb of arousal all over again. Chase had let go of her hands at some point, and she gripped Zach's shoulders while he pounded her pussy relentlessly. This wasn't a seduction, but a claiming. She reveled in his passion, lost in her own. He shifted the stroke a little until he was rubbing the sweet spot inside of her.

"She likes that, Zach. Keep that up, she's really close."

Chase pinched her nipples, and Zach pinched her already sensitive clit. It sent her into another orgasm, stronger than the last. Her pussy clamped down on Zach's cock. He pounded her as he, too, reached the peak, stilling inside her. His eyes were closed in ecstasy, his face twisted as if in pain. He was still for a few moments before regretfully withdrawing. He leaned down to kiss her long and slow, a stark contrast to his raw passion only moments before. "Chase's turn, angel." Zach whispered and changed places with his brother.

Chase grinned down at her as he opened his jeans and donned a condom. She smiled back. This was her playful, teasing Chase. He eased slowly into her pussy until he was balls deep. She moaned at the fullness. His cock ran along already sensitive spots in her swollen cunt.

Her senses were heightened. She could smell the distinct, spicy scents of her men, the earthy smell of the barn. She felt their rough, callused hands caress her and heard Chase grunt with the each stroke.

He withdrew almost all the way, and then plunged back in. His cock bumped her cervix sending arousal shooting to her clit. In and out, he fucked her, harder with every stroke. She tightened her muscles around Chase's cock, and he groaned in response.

They were covered in sweat as he rode her cunt hard and fast. She moaned as his fingers played with her clit. She didn't think she could come again, but Chase was determined. His expression was a study in control. She knew he was holding back for her.

"I can't, Chase. You go ahead." She panted for air.

"No, dammit. You're coming again. Zach, help her." Chase's voice was rough with passion. She knew he was holding on by a thread. Zach leaned over and sucked on her nipple hard, pulling it into his mouth and biting down with his teeth. The edge of pain sent her over and she screamed her orgasm, bucking against Zach's hold. Chase finally let himself go and slammed into her one last time before holding himself inside her. His cock pulsed inside her sending ripples throughout her cunt. Finally, he collapsed on top of her, gasping for breath.

Zach kissed her neck and pushed at Chase. "You're squashing our girl."

Chase sat up and grinned. "Sorry, baby. That was intense makeup sex."

Cassie couldn't hold back her own grin. "Wow. It certainly was. I've never had makeup sex before."

Zach smirked. "Stick with us, angel. We're sure to piss you off on a regular basis, so makeup sex is a given."

As long as she got to win the arguments, Cassie didn't mind. She loved these men, and they loved her. Her past seemed very far away now.

Chapter 11

"Prisoner 87433, move to the yellow line!"

Danny Trent stepped forward, through his cell door, and onto the yellow line. He was being transferred today from county jail to state prison. He was surprised it was happening at all due to the state prison overcrowding. His attorney had assured him that if he behaved well that he had a good chance of getting to stay in county, which was much nicer than the state accommodations. Danny had made himself into the model prisoner, but his fucking attorney turned out to also be a fucking liar. He was being transferred today, and there was nothing he could do about it. It was the second worst thing about being locked up—not having any control over his life. He was told when to get up, when to eat, when to piss, and when to sleep. Now he was being told he was going to Logan, and he had heard bad things about that place. He wasn't too popular in county as it was since they said he had terrorized a woman, but in state, he was told he would only be a rung above the child molesters. Somehow, he had to stop this from happening. Then he had to fix the worst thing about being locked up. He was away from Cassandra. God, he missed her. Her golden hair and blue eyes. He loved her so much, and it was killing him each and every day to be away from her.

"87433, step three steps to your right!"

Danny stepped three steps to his right and met one of the guards at that spot. The guard looked at him dispassionately and snapped handcuffs on his right wrist, drew his arm behind his back and then snapped his left wrist in a cuff. Bastard cop. He had snapped them tight, too. Danny could feel the metal pressing into his flesh as he pulled against them. It was instinct. He couldn't seem to stop himself.

"87433, we are here to transfer you to Logan Correctional Center where you will serve the balance of your sentence which is four and a half years. Officer O'Halloran here will collect your belongings and you will be escorted to the van waiting downstairs."

Danny watched as the officer took a small garbage bag and began to collect his books, letters, and a few clothes.

O'Halloran didn't look at the guard as he gathered up Danny's belongings, so Danny was surprised when he spoke.

"You need to get the prisoner in manacles for travel. Handcuffs are not sufficient for transfer."

"We do that in the holding area, O'Halloran. It upsets the other prisoners to see manacles, so we don't do that in general population."

O'Halloran rolled his eyes at the guard. "Well, we wouldn't want to upset them now, would we?"

Some of the letters and books slipped from O'Halloran's hand and landed on the floor with a plop. Papers fluttered to the floor and Danny looked in horror as the picture of Cassandra floated out from one of the books and fell on O'Halloran's shoe.

"Well, what have we here, Trent? This can't be a picture of Miss Cassandra Ames. I believe you were instructed by the judge that you could not have any pictures of your *victim*. This is a clear violation, Danny boy. Looks like you head straight for solitary when we get to Logan. A few weeks in the hole ought to straighten your head right out. Oh, and this will erase any good behavior points you may have banked. Yep, looks like you will be serving the whole five years, Trent. I'll make sure the guards keep an extra special eye on you from now on."

Danny felt the heat of his anger as he saw O'Halloran smirk at him. God, he hated fucking cops, and especially this cop. O'Halloran had been the detective on his case and had testified at the trial. He wanted to beat the shit out of him and wipe that smirk off his face. He just couldn't spend the next four and a half years in Logan. He would die first. Danny spit at the cop.

"Fuck you, O'Halloran. I'll see you in hell before I serve all fucking five years in that shit hole."

O'Halloran grabbed one of Danny's socks and wiped the spit off of his tie with a grin then threw it in the trash bag with Danny's other things.

"I guess we'll see, Trent. I remember you that day when you beat up that young woman, and it doesn't appear that you're any smarter now than then. I think you're going to spend a lot of time in solitary. You know, my whole career I've been dealing with sick fucks like you. Guys that think that rules don't apply to them. But the rules do apply. You did terrible things to that woman, and she deserves peace in her life, and you deserve a hell of a lot more than the judge sentenced you to. Me? I just want to be sure that Cassandra Ames gets justice and the taxpayers get their money's worth for the next four and a half years."

O'Halloran quickly finished gathering up the few possessions that Danny still had and gave the guard the sign that they were ready to move. Danny walked between them down the hall and out of the general population area. Some of the prisoners called to them as they exited, but Danny wasn't listening. His mind was whirling. He had to find a way to stop this from happening. He couldn't end up in Logan. He just couldn't. A wave of anger overtook him. It was Cassandra's fault that this was happening. If she hadn't disobeyed, he wouldn't have had to punish her and he wouldn't be here. She really had another punishment coming to her, and he didn't want to wait five years to give it to her. She needed to learn to obey and respect him. He couldn't allow this to happen.

They arrived at the van, and O'Halloran's phone rang.

"What? Yeah? Well, shit? All right, I'll be there in about twenty." O'Halloran hung up and turned to the armed driver of the van. "This guard will be accompanying Trent to Logan. I have to go interrogate a suspect that was just apprehended."

Danny saw the prison guard gape and start to protest. "I can't go to Logan, Detective. I'm supposed to take my girlfriend to a Halloween party."

"Sorry, man. Looks like you get overtime today. Someone needs to accompany Trent to Logan, and I just got called back to central. Just sit back, and enjoy the drive. I'll call Logan and let them know the change. Oh, and I will let them know about Trent's victim violation." He gave Danny a serene smile. "I am sure they will want to deal with that first thing when he arrives at his new home."

The guard relented. "Okay, I could use the OT anyway. My girlfriend wants to go to Vegas."

"See there. Look at this like a bonus. A little babysitting job that you get paid for. So get him in manacles and ready to travel."

O'Halloran smirked at Danny. "I'll come see you in a few weeks when you get out of the hole, Trent."

* * * *

Cassie whirled around in front of the mirror with a laugh. Her Halloween costume was going to knock her boys out of their socks. She had chosen a stewardess costume at the Halloween store in Tampa, and she loved how sexy it made her feel. Of course, the last month with her guys made her feel sexy and loved all the time. They went to movies, played bingo, cooked, talked, biked from the park to the historic district, and of course, made love. Whether she was with one of them or both of them, they made her feel beautiful and sexy.

She couldn't ever remember being this happy. From the gossip at Becca's shop, Cassie had heard that Amelia had high-tailed it back to Dallas. Her father was not happy about her abrupt departure. By the scowls that Zach and Chase had received from him in the diner, Ambrose Winters blamed them. He was a prominent man in town and could make trouble for Zach and Chase's construction business, but they had been adamant that Cassie's feelings were more important than business.

"Your Halloween costume is going to knock Zach and Chase on their asses," Jillian said.

"Do really think so? I feel so sexy in it."

"You look sexy in it," Rebecca said as she adjusted the nurse's cap on her head. She was dressed as a naughty nurse. Jillian rounded out the trio with her schoolgirl costume with its plaid skirt, white blouse, knee socks, patent leather shoes, and pigtails.

"My brothers are going to have a heart attack when they see you, Jillian. You look to die for in that schoolgirl costume. Hell, we all look to die for." Rebecca laughed as she grabbed her camera and started snapping pictures of the three of them in their costumes.

Jillian frowned at Rebecca. "I am not trying to get Ryan and Jackson's attention. I told you that I don't do relationships."

"And I told you that you haven't seen my brothers when they are determined…and believe me, they are very determined that you give them a chance. They are nice guys, Jillian. And they really, really like you."

"I like them, too, Rebecca. They seem like great guys. But tonight, I just want to have fun, okay? No trying to fix me up with your brothers. Deal?"

"Deal. But that doesn't mean they won't try, or I won't try on another night." Rebecca smirked.

Jillian grabbed her telephone and moved in front of the other two girls. "I want to send a picture of you two to my brother in Chicago. He's a doctor, and he's going to love your nurse outfit, Rebecca."

Jillian snapped a picture of Cassie and Rebecca and quickly sent the picture to her brother in Chicago.

"I didn't know you had a brother. He's really a doctor?"

"Yeah, he's some big deal surgeon in Chicago. He's older than me and has been married for several years to a great guy. Travis is a lawyer."

"All the good ones are taken. Is he as good-looking as you are?"

"Mark is much better looking than I am. He looks a lot like my mother while I look more like our dad. His husband is even hotter than he is."

Jillian's phone suddenly vibrated and started playing a dance tune from the eighties. "Look! A reply from Mark already! He says he loves the picture, especially the sexy nurse. What's her name?"

"He so did not say that!" Rebecca turned a faint shade of pink.

"You can see for yourself, Rebecca. He thinks you look hot. He also asked how you're doing, Cassie. I've been telling him about you, Zach, and Chase."

Cassie groaned. "I can't believe you've been telling your brother that I'm dating two men. How incredibly embarrassing. He must think I'm a total slut."

"No, he just thinks you're one lucky woman. Both he and Travis think that's pretty hot, you doing two guys."

"I am not *doing* two guys, Jillian. I am in a *relationship* with two guys. Don't make it sound cheap."

"Tomato, tomahto. Either way, Cass, there are two men in your bed."

Cassie decided to change the subject. "Rebecca, tell us more about the limestone quarries."

"Limestone has been mined for years in Florida. The party is going to be held at the old limestone quarry just north of town. Haven't you guys biked out there yet?"

"No, we haven't biked that far yet."

"Well it's really beautiful there with the lake and all. It's a great place to have the Halloween party. We don't have to worry about how much noise we make. Ryan will show up just to make sure that nobody's driving drunk. But other than that you can't get into much trouble at the quarries. Well, I guess except for the lake."

"What do you mean by trouble at the lake?" Jillian knitted her brow in question.

"The lake area is beautiful, but it can be dangerous if you're not familiar with the area," Rebecca replied with a shrug.

"How so?" Jillian asked.

"One side of the lake has a twenty-foot drop from the road. It was left there when they finished the mining, and no one has ever gone back to do anything about it. There really isn't a reason to since all the locals know to be careful around that curve of road."

Cassie and Jillian both laughed, and Jillian said, "Well, just make sure that we know where that curve of road is so we don't fall into the lake."

Cassie heard a truck in the driveway and realized the boys had finally arrived.

"The boys are here. We better grab our stuff and get out there. You know how impatient they are."

* * * *

The prison van headed south on I-55. Danny knew they were less than an hour from Logan, and he felt helpless to stop what was happening. It was almost dusk, and soon they would be arriving at the prison where the state of Illinois expected him to live for the next four and a half years. Danny couldn't fathom being away from Cassandra for that long. He would never live through it.

He glanced across the seat to the guard accompanying him to Logan. Danny had never liked him all that much in the county lockup, but at least the dumb fuck hadn't remembered to put the manacles on him. Consequently, Danny was able to stretch his legs out and be comfortable. Well, as comfortable as he could be with his wrists in handcuffs that were locked to the door next to him. Maybe this guard was dumb enough to unlock his cuffs.

"So you were supposed to go to a Halloween party tonight, huh?"

The guard looked up, vaguely surprised that Danny had spoken. He hadn't spoken the entire trip so far. "Yeah, she was pretty pissed. You know how women can be."

"Yeah, I do. That's why I am here, you know."

The guard's eyes narrowed at Danny. "I heard different, Trent. Heard you beat up that woman and killed her dog. I like dogs."

Danny smiled his most charming smile. He knew it worked most of the time with women and this guard was almost as stupid as a woman.

"It was all a misunderstanding. She likes it rough, ya know? Some chicks dig getting slapped around a little."

The guard looked like he might believe him and was about to reply when the van swerved and began to bump and roll, knocking him out of his seat and slamming him against the door. *Fuck!* Danny looked out the front and saw that a huge deer was running off into the woods. The driver must have swerved to avoid hitting it. Finally, the van came to a stop, upside down. The guard moaned and blinked several times as he opened his eyes. Blood rolled down his forehead and into his eyes. Danny saw confusion on the guard's face and knew he had his chance.

"Help me, man. I think my arm is broken. It got twisted in the cuffs when we rolled over."

The guard shook his head a little to clear it and moved forward to check the driver, who was slumped over the steering wheel. His eyes went wide, and Danny saw fear. Fear—even better.

"Shit. He's dead, I think. I can't feel a pulse. Oh God!"

"Please, man. My arm hurts so bad. It must be busted from the cuffs. Don't let me die like that guy." Danny moaned a few times and closed his eyes as if in pain. He didn't need to pretend too much as his ribs hurt like a son of a bitch. But his ribs weren't in handcuffs. First things first.

"Yeah, hold on. Let me get you unlocked. Are you hurt anywhere else?"

"Yeah, I think I hurt my back and ribs, too, but mostly my arm. Please, hurry!" Danny moaned again as the guard quickly unlocked the cuffs.

"I'll just get on the radio and call for help."

Danny stood up as much as he could in the cramped space and kicked the guard in the head as hard as he could. The guard stumbled back and groaned.

"Sorry, man. Can't let you call anyone. And thanks for forgetting to put manacles on me. It's going to make this so much easier."

Danny punched and kicked the guard until he was unconscious. Knowing he only had moments before help arrived, he quickly swapped clothes with the guard and handcuffed him to the door as Danny had been only five minutes before. He grabbed the guard's wallet and gun and headed out into the ever darkening night. He and Cassandra would be together forever.

Chapter 12

The party was in full swing when the group arrived. Pumpkin lanterns were strung everywhere, casting an orange glow beneath the trees. Spiderwebs were strung from tree to tree, and fake blood dripped down tree trunks. Skeletons and ghosts were hung from branches and blew in the wind. To top it all off, there were several fog machines sending rolls of billowing mist at the partygoers' feet. It all added up to a very festive scene.

Chase nodded to the townsfolk as they moved through the crowd. Cassie had loved his pirate costume and said he looked very rakish, and he was glad to see that his costume was one of the more conservative at the party. There were pirates, harem girls, football players, vampires, and what looked like an Imperial Stormtrooper. Even Zach, who hated parties, seemed to be enjoying himself in his cowboy costume. If they had known that Cassie was dressing up as a stewardess, they would've dressed up as airline pilots, but she had insisted on keeping it a secret until tonight. She sure did look sexy, and Chase was wondering how long they would have to stay at the party before they could get her home and into their bed.

He and Zach thought about Cassie all the time, even when they were working. They couldn't seem to get enough of her. They liked the way she was so funny and so smart, and she seemed to make everything better without even trying. He had always thought that letting a woman into his life would mean giving up something. But with Cassie, she added to his life instead. Since meeting her, they had certainly found lots in common. They all three liked being outdoors and going for bike rides. Cassie liked cooking at home and watching movies, and he and Zach found that just doing these simple things with her were special. Some nights, Cassie had papers to grade, and he and Zach would play pool while she finished her schoolwork. All three of them would then curl up in the big master bedroom often to make love and sometimes just sleep. Even when they just slept, he was more content than he had ever been just to hold Cassie all night long. He loved the life they were building together. Rebecca's soft voice interrupted his daydreaming.

"Jackson, about time you got here. I was worried you weren't coming."

Chase saw Jackson Parks heading toward them in a Ghostbusters costume and a big grin. Jackson loved Halloween and had dragged Ryan, Zach, and himself out every year since they were kids. Of course, when they were kids they soaped windows and hung toilet paper from trees. Then as teenagers, they had taken their dates out onto the spooky, deserted roads hoping to do a little "parking" with the girls. "No way, little sister. I wouldn't miss the Halloween party for anything. You know I have spiderwebs in my blood."

Chase saw Jackson give Jillian that once-over and gulp at her schoolgirl costume. Yep, Jack and Ryan were really gone over Jillian. She was a nice girl but seemed to be giving them a run for their money. He wasn't sure that Jackson had ever been turned down by a woman in his life. He might be getting ready to find out what it was like.

Jackson turned to Jillian. "Care to dance, Jillian?"

Jillian turned a bright red and seemed to have trouble breathing. Ah yes, Jillian liked them, too. Why was she fighting it?

"Well, I...um...don't dance much..."

Jackson grinned and took the advantage. "I'll take that as a yes. Come on, sweetheart." Jackson led Jillian into the dance area as the DJ started playing a slow tune. Chase smiled at Jackson's guts. He had to admire a man who wouldn't take maybe for an answer.

Chase turned to Cassie. "How about you and I taking a turn?"

Cassie turned her head a little as if to say, "What about Rebecca?" and luckily Zach caught on quickly.

"How about you and me, Becca? We'll show them who the best dancer is in the Harper family."

* * * *

Cassie was having a great time at the party. She had danced with Chase and Zach all evening and even with Jackson Parks. Everyone made sure that she, Jillian, and Rebecca had a great time. Jillian seemed to be warming up a little to Jack, and Rebecca had turned the heads of several young men.

As she circled the dance floor with Chase, Cassie closed her eyes and breathed in his warm, masculine scent. She snuggled closer to his muscular chest and felt his arms tighten around her.

"What are you thinking about, Cassie? You have a very evil little smile on your face." Cassie felt Chase's chest rumble with laughter.

Cassie looked up into Chase's handsome face. She wondered if she would ever get over how handsome he was.

"Well, evil thoughts to go with my evil smile, Chase. Isn't Halloween a night to have evil thoughts?"

"Hmmm…I would hate for Zach and I to have to punish you for those evil thoughts." Chase waggled his eyebrows and grinned.

"Punishment?" Cassie felt her cream flood her pussy at the thought of a punishment from her men. It was hardly real punishment. It was more like *pleasurement*. Was that even a word? It should be with these two.

"Yes, Cassie, punishment. Zach and I don't want to have to spank your cute little bottom and keep you from coming for a couple of hours. But if we have to, we will." He sighed an exaggerated sigh.

Cassie batted her eyelashes playfully at him. "You wouldn't keep me from coming that long, Chase. You couldn't stand it. Zach could, but not you. You are too sweet."

"Is that a challenge? Because a Harper man never backs down from a challenge, sweetheart."

Before Cassie could answer, Zach came up behind her and nuzzled her neck. "I think it might be time to go home and play a little trick and treat."

"Don't you mean trick or treat, Zach?"

"No, ma'am. I want all tricks and all treats." Zach grinned and bit her ear a little playfully.

The mention of treats made Cassie feel a little hungry, and she was just about to suggest a trip to the buffet table when she heard Zach call out to someone.

"Hey, Ryan! What kind costume is that?"

Cassie turned to see Ryan Parks walking toward them in his sheriff uniform.

"I'm dressed up as law enforcement, Zach. Not that anyone would listen to me tonight anyway."

"Don't tell me you got stuck working tonight?"

"Yeah, one of my deputies called in sick. But, I'm just as glad that I was on duty tonight anyway."

Jillian, Jackson, and Becca must have spied Ryan's arrival. The seven of them congregated away from the music where they could talk more easily.

Ryan slapped his little brother on the back and then gave his sister a hug. Jackson grinned.

"I've been wondering where you were, bro. I had to dance with the pretty lady all by myself tonight."

Ryan looked at Jillian and smiled a regretful smile. "Well, duty called, bro. But I actually need to talk to Cassie. It's important."

Cassie looked into Ryan's eyes and saw they were guarded as if he was trying not to show any emotion. A sick feeling started in her stomach. She had seen that look in an officer's eyes before. Right before they told her something she didn't want to hear, to be exact.

"Sheriff, I don't think I want to hear what you have to tell me."

"I wish I wasn't here, too, Cassie. But I'm afraid I have some very bad news."

Cassie grabbed on to Zach and Chase for support. They each put an arm around her and pulled her a little closer.

"Ryan, you better tell us what the fuck you're doing here tonight. You're scaring Cassie." Zach's voice was tight with tension.

Cassie felt Zach's arm tighten around her shoulders in comfort. She knew what the sheriff had to say wasn't going to be pleasant, and she steeled herself for the news.

"I just got a call from the Chicago PD. It seems that Danny Trent was being transferred from county lockup to state prison today. There was some sort of accident, and Danny Trent has escaped. The driver of the van was killed in the accident, and the other officer was badly injured when Trent escaped. Trent almost beat him to death, stole his clothes, gun, and wallet, and has disappeared."

Cassie felt dizzy as she processed his words. This couldn't be happening. Danny was supposed to be put away for five years. She wasn't supposed to have to worry about this for five fucking years. She just kept hearing the words over and over again—he escaped. He escaped. He escaped.

"Don't worry, Cassie. No one's going to get near you. Zach and I will protect you. We told you we always take care of our own."

Cassie looked up into Chase's face and saw the anger she had seen the night she told them about Danny. His jaw was tight and his eyes narrow. She reached up and tried to smooth away the lines in his forehead. He turned his face slightly and kissed her palm. She saw his eyes soften a little. She turned to Zach and tried to give him a brave smile. Zach smiled grimly and turned to Ryan.

"So what are the Chicago police doing, Ryan? Are they close to catching him? Do we know where he's headed?"

Before Ryan could answer, Jillian answered for him. "Let me guess, Sheriff. Chicago PD has no clue where Danny is, where he's headed, or how far he's gotten? Am I correct?"

Cassie recognized the bitterness in Jillian's voice. She had always felt badly that Jillian had to go through this with her. It hadn't been fair to Jillian, and here they were again. No one knew better than Jillian and herself how inept the Chicago PD could be when it came to finding Danny Trent. Big cities had bigger problems than stalkers. Their resources were already stretched thin chasing murderers, drug dealers, and gang bangers.

"Yes, Jillian, you are correct. I'm sorry to say the Chicago PD have no clue were Danny Trent is or where he might be heading. But I will promise you this—the Plenty Police Department will protect you with their lives. Both of you. If Trent shows his face in this town, we'll get him."

Jackson put his arm around Jillian in comfort. Cassie noticed that Jillian leaned into him as if seeking his strength.

"My brother is right, Jillian. No one is going to get near you or Cassie. We take care of our own here in Plenty. Besides, this is a small town and, as you know, newcomers stand out. There's no way Trent can hang around this town without being noticed."

The Sheriff nodded grimly. Cassie could see that Sheriff Ryan was frustrated and seemed quite pissed off.

"I've notified all my deputies about Trent and passed his picture around. If he shows his face anywhere, we'll recognize him. But honestly, the chances of him making it all the way to Florida are remote. We've already put a trace on the officer's credit cards. If Trent uses them, we'll be able to find out where he is. According to the officer, he had less than one hundred dollars in that wallet. Trent won't get far on one hundred dollars. In the meantime, I think you and Jillian should stay with Zach and Chase. They have an excellent security system and they can keep an eye on you until we catch Trent."

"Ryan's right. You and Jillian can stay with Zach and me. We have a state-of-the-art security system that we put in when the house was built but never had a reason to use until now."

Cassie shook her head. "I don't want to put you guys in danger. You don't know what this guy is capable of. I do. He almost killed that officer today. He won't hesitate to kill you to get to me. Jillian should stay with you so she'll be safe."

Jillian started to protest. "Fuck no, Cassie. He's not going to go after me. He never had any interest in hurting me, only you."

The sheriff held up his hand to halt the conversation. "Stop. You are both going to go to Zach and Chase's house where I know you will stay safe. I don't want to have to be worrying about the two of you while we're out looking for Trent." The sheriff turned toward his brother.

"Jack, I want you to help Zach and Chase keep Jillian and Cassie safe. Take shifts if you need to, and never leave them alone."

"Will do, bro. Where will you be?"

"My deputies and I will be patrolling the area and also staying in touch with Chicago PD for any updates. I have my cell, so you can always get a hold of me. Listen to me, Cassie. I know you don't know me very well, and you have no reason to trust me, but believe me when I tell you that this town is the very safest place for you right now. This sick bastard from the city doesn't stand a chance in a town full of good old boy Florida crackers who pretty much all own a gun or two, or six for that matter. That guy's going to be plenty sorry that he ever came to this town."

"Damn straight, bro. No pansy-assed stalker is going to get by us. Ryan and I will protect our woman and her best friend."

An incredulous look crossed Jillian's face. "And who the hell would be your woman? I know you don't mean Cassie, and you sure as hell don't mean me."

Jillian crossed her arms over her chest and glared at the handsome firefighter and his brother. Despite the seriousness of the situation, Cassie couldn't help but be amused at Jillian's anger and the brothers' obvious discomfort.

"I sure as hell do mean you. Ryan and I have made no secret that we're after you, so it will come as no surprise to you that we want to keep you safe. If you have issues with it, we'll deal with that at another time. Right now the most important thing is keeping you and Cassie safe."

Jackson Parks scowled with frustration at Jillian's glare. However, unlike the other men Jillian had dated, he didn't look in the least like he was going to back down. If anything, he looked more determined than ever. Cassie couldn't help but think about the other men Jillian had dated and how they had allowed themselves to be cowed by Jillian's anger.

Sheriff Ryan dragged his hand down his face as he shook his head at his brother and Jillian. "There will be lots of time in the future to discuss our relationship and how we all feel about each other. But Jack is right about this. Neither Jack nor I am going to let anyone hurt you or Cassie. I know Zach and Chase feel the same way."

Cassie's men nodded, and she was a little alarmed at the look in their eyes. It was at that moment that Cassie saw the man that Zach used to be—that Navy SEAL. He probably knew a couple hundred ways to kill a man. Heck, he probably had killed a man before, and looking into his eyes right now, he certainly looked like he wouldn't mind doing it again.

Chapter 13

It was a silent ride back to the condo. Cassie cuddled close to Chase in the front seat while Jillian sat in the back seat with Jackson and Becca. No one seemed to have much to say as they pulled into the driveway and came to a stop. Chase untangled himself from Cassie and helped her out of the SUV. Zach was at her side instantly, lending another helping hand. Cassie smiled gratefully at her men and glanced back at Jillian and Becca. Jillian's lips were tight in what Cassie knew was a very pissed-off state. Whether she was in that state because of Jackson's earlier declaration or the situation that Danny's escape had put them in was anyone's guess. Cassie saw Becca put her arm around Jillian when Jillian had shrugged off Jackson's arm. Jackson looked as pissed off as Jillian did, and Becca was trying to play the peacemaker. Good luck to her. Jillian had a temper to match her red hair, and tonight's little episode wasn't going to help much.

Becca had already agreed to stay the night at the farm with Cassie and Jillian. Jackson and Ryan didn't want Becca alone tonight after hearing the news. Cassie noticed that Becca had looked a little annoyed at first, but after looking at Jillian's tight features she had readily agreed. Becca was turning out to be a really good friend to them both. Jackson put his arm around Becca and gave her a hug.

"Zach, I'll take Becca to her place to get some clothes while you help Jillian and Cassie."

"Thanks, Jack. We'll meet you back here at the truck in just a few minutes, okay?"

Cassie silently followed Zach and Chase as they unlocked her front door and started turning on lights. Danny had only escaped hours before, but Cassie couldn't help looking around her condo quickly for any signs that he had been there. Of course there were none, and she felt the surge of anger that had been simmering since the sheriff had given her the news.

"I know that look, Cassie. You're pissed." As usual, Jillian had figured her out in seconds.

"Pissed is too weak a work, Jill. I am beyond fucking pissed!" Cassie threw her purse on the table and let out a yell. "Arrr!"

"That's it girl, yell! Let it out!" Jillian looked ready to join in her mini-tirade.

Chase and Zach came rushing to her side to hug her and try to calm her down.

"It's okay, sweetheart. Calm down. No one is going to get near you with Zach and me here."

"I don't want to fucking calm down, Chase. I want to be pissed. Just for a little while anyway. I am mad. Mad! Danny has had way too much power over my life as it is, and now he gets to have more of it! I am sick and tired of this! I am tired of looking over my fucking shoulder! I am tired of being fucking afraid not just for me, but for my friends, too. It isn't fucking fair, and I want to be mad for a few minutes. After that, I promise, I will calm down and act mature. But right now I am pissed as hell!"

Jillian looked amused at her outburst while Zach and Chase's mouths hung open. Apparently, they had never seen her this wound up. Well, there was no time like the present to find out she had a bit of a temper, too.

Zach was the first to recover and start laughing. "Well, I didn't know my angel could say that many F-words in just a few sentences. Go ahead, Cassie, be mad if you need to be. Chase and I will clean up anything you need to break or throw."

Chase grinned. "Hell yeah! I might even join you if throwing stuff is involved."

Jillian looked at Cassie with a big smile. "Yep, those two are keepers, Cass. Now let's get our stuff and get out of here. I am exhausted."

Cassie let out a loud sigh and let her arms drop to her sides. "Me, too, Jillian."

* * * *

Zach stared out the large kitchen window. Their driveway was lit but anything beyond was pitch black. Zach now wished they had gotten around to installing more lighting down the long driveway. The house was a couple of miles from town and the streetlights didn't come out this far.

While the women were putting their things away and getting ready for bed, Zach saw Ryan pull up in the driveway. Chase noticed, too, and started to say something, but Zach put his finger up to his lips. He didn't want the women to hear anything. They were upset enough as it was, and besides, Zach wanted to talk to Ryan privately. He stepped outside before Ryan had a chance to come into the house. This would give him the privacy he needed to ask the Sheriff a few questions.

"Have you heard anything new, Ryan?" Zach could see the grim set of the sheriff's jaw and steeled himself for bad news.

"The Chicago PD haven't found him yet if that's what you're asking, Zach. I wish I had better news. It's like he disappeared into thin air. But the police have been questioning some of Trent's acquaintances. Seems that one of them told him that Cassie moved to Florida, for Christ's sake. Apparently, this guy didn't think Trent was dangerous or anything. He didn't think he would break out of prison." Zach could hear the sarcasm in Ryan's voice and felt the same frustration.

"You mean that Trent knows she's here. *Fuck*." The sound of Chase's fist landing against the garage door made both men turn.

"Cut it out, Chase. That isn't going to help anything." Ryan's voice was tight with anger. Zach could tell that Ryan was as pissed off as they were.

"Listen, we need to keep the women safe. I don't trust this Trent not to show up here and do something really stupid. This guy is crazy and violent. Did Cassie tell you what all he did up there?"

"Yeah, she said he killed her dog and attacked her in a parking garage. A Grade-A asshole and loony tune."

"Zach, I hate to tell you, but it sounds like Cassie cleaned up the story a little for you and Chase." Zach could see Ryan sigh and look down. This didn't sound good, and he could see Chase had stopped pacing the driveway to listen.

"I talked to the Chicago PD. Trent is violent, all right. He killed Cassie's dog and hung the body on the front door for her to find. He did call her repeatedly, that much is true. But what it sounds like she didn't tell you is that he threatened to kill her. If he couldn't have her, then no one would. He said that he would shoot Cassie and then shoot himself, so they would be together in heaven for eternity.

"When he found her in that parking garage, he damned near killed her. She was in the hospital for a week with a concussion, broken ribs, broken arm, broken collarbone, and broken ankle. He was dragging her to his car when the cops got there. She fought like a wildcat, too. That's why she got so hurt. She wasn't going quietly. The police found several knives, a gun, rope, and plastic bags in the trunk of Trent's car. That's not all either. At the trial, Trent would scream during the proceedings that he loved Cassie and that she needed to be punished. That she belonged to him for all of eternity.

"When he was taken away after sentencing, they had to sedate him because he was struggling and screaming to get to Cassie. There is no doubt in my mind that he will come here to find her. We have to keep her and Jillian safe from this asshole."

Zach's mind reeled at all that his woman had been through. Primitive instincts as old as time welled up in him. He would protect Cassie with his life. Jillian, too. No one would get near them. He would make sure of that. He looked at Ryan, one of his oldest friends, and crossed his arms. Let's get this party started, he thought. That old familiar feeling he used to get before a mission was tight in his gut.

"So what's the plan, Ryan? Sounds like it is only a matter of time before Trent gets here."

"Wait, Zach." Chase held up his hand. "I thought Ryan said that Trent had less than a hundred bucks and it was unlikely he could make it here."

Zach could hear the hope in Chase's voice. He knew that he would have to dash that hope with his next words, but Ryan did it for him.

"I only said that so Cassie wouldn't freak out. The fact is, a man like Trent doesn't need money. He will steal whatever he needs to make it down here, whether it is a car or money. I say we probably have another twelve to sixteen hours before he gets here. We need to start making plans now."

"Shit! Fuck!" Chase yelled, and Zach had to quiet him so Cassie wouldn't hear inside the house. Despite his easygoing nature, Chase was the hothead of the two of them, and Zach knew he needed to make sure Chase stayed in control.

"Cool it, Chase. We have to keep it together for Cassie. We don't have the luxury of getting angry."

"Sorry, bro. But when I think about what that asshole did to Cassie." Chase's jaw snapped shut and his color was high.

"I know, but we can get angry later—after Trent is behind bars again."

Ryan sat heavily in one of the lawn chairs with a sigh. "Part one of the plan—we need to never let the women alone. They aren't going to like it much, but this time, he just might kill her if we turn our backs for even a second. He has nothing to lose except her. I already called the principal at the school, and Cassie and Jillian will have substitutes until this is all over. I don't want to take a chance that Trent might take a hostage or two when she is around the kids. They need to stay in the house with the alarm on at all times. I will keep a deputy patrolling the area, but one of you or Jack should be here with the women. Part two of the plan—do you need any ammunition?"

Zach shook his head with a grimace. "No. You know we keep several guns in the gun safe along with plenty of ammunition. The dads were always ready for Armageddon, you know." He jerked his head toward the east of the property where his parents lived.

He thanked God that they were up in Georgia right now visiting relatives. They would be out of the way if anything happened. He didn't need to worry about them, too.

"Trent will stick out like a sore thumb when he shows up here. No way will he be able to hide in plain sight, so to speak. We'll get him when he gets here."

* * * *

Cassie snuggled into the down comforter and stared up at the ceiling in Zach's room. Jillian was asleep in Chase's room, and Becca was asleep in the guestroom. She knew Jackson was also going to spend the night on the couch. Zach and Chase had disappeared outside earlier and hadn't returned to the house yet. She sighed as she turned over and tried to find a comfortable spot, knowing that she probably wouldn't fall asleep anyway. An evening that had started out so promising had turned into her worst nightmare. She still felt a little numb at the news that Danny had escaped and was probably headed there. All she and Jillian had wanted was a fresh start in a new place.

"Cassie? Are you asleep, honey?" Zach's voice broke into her maudlin thoughts.

"No. I don't think I will be sleeping for a while. Not until Danny's caught." Cassie sighed at how pathetic she sounded. She hated being anything other than strong and in control. This just sucked, and she was really sick and tired of it. What must Zach and Chase be thinking now? Would they think she was too much trouble? They certainly didn't sign on for all these issues. Maybe they were wishing they had never gotten involved with her in the first place. Perhaps Amelia, even with all her self-absorbed bullshit, was looking better than Cassie right now? Acting pathetic was really starting to piss her off.

"Well, we will see what we can do about that, angel. Chase and I are going to hold you all night long so you feel safe. You will always be safe with us here to take care of you."

"You shouldn't have to take care of me, dammit! You shouldn't have to keep me safe from anything. Crazy, psycho killers are not supposed to be after me, and I am supposed to be able to take care of myself. I am pissed off, and I want my life back. Don't you hate this, too? Doesn't it piss you off that you have to do this? I hate that I have issues, so you must hate this, too."

Cassie buried her head in the pillow and groaned, but Zach just pulled her up into his arms and on his lap. She was surprised to see Chase slide in next to him and stroke his hands in circles on her lower back. She felt herself slowly relaxing in their strong, warm arms. Her head fell back onto Chase's shoulder, and she closed her eyes as she felt some of her tension drain away.

"We don't hate this, and we like taking care of you. What we do hate is that you have to go through this again," said Zach. He nuzzled her neck, and she breathed in his masculine, spicy scent. She really did feel safe when she was with the two of them. She knew they would protect her no matter what.

She felt Zach lift her and place her between the two of them, tucking her into the nook of his shoulder. Chase cuddled to her back, placing tiny kisses along the back of her neck.

"Zach and I are here for you, sweetheart. We will always love and protect you. So close those beautiful, blue eyes, and try and get a little sleep. We will be right here if you need us."

Cassie closed her eyes as Chase traced hypnotic circles on her stomach, lulling her into a blessedly dreamless sleep.

Chapter 14

Danny looked out the window of the farmhouse, sweeping his gaze from left to right looking for any indication that police were in the vicinity. He had found this deserted farmhouse outside of Bourbonnais, and so far, it seemed to be fairly safe. The police would be expecting him to head straight for Florida and Cassandra. It would be safer to hide out here for a few days until they assumed he was out of the state and stopped looking for him. And they would eventually stop looking for him. The state didn't have enough money to keep a manhunt going for days.

Luckily, the inhabitants of the farmhouse appeared to have not been gone that long. There was still some nonperishable food in the cabinets and basic furniture in the house. He wouldn't starve, and he wouldn't die from exposure. Danny couldn't help but think that this was all Cassandra's fault. If he hadn't had to punish her then he wouldn't have been arrested and now running from the cops. Sometimes he felt more anger than love for her. He knew that, once he punished her for all that had happened, the anger would fade, and he would just feel love. He loved her more than anyone and anything, and she needed to understand that and appreciate him more. That was really the problem. She didn't appreciate all he had been through and done for her. He would help her understand that he was the only person that truly loved her and would always take care of her.

Just a few more days, Cassandra, and we will be together forever.

* * * *

Cassie sipped at her coffee and stared out of the kitchen window while Jillian was at the stove making French toast. They didn't have anywhere to be today. Substitute teachers had taken over their classes, and despite her frustration with the situation, Cassie couldn't argue that it was the best thing for the kids. She didn't want them to be in any danger, and anyone around her was probably not safe. Danny would be desperate, and there was no telling what he might do. In the weeks before his arrest, his behavior had escalated, and she had no reason to believe that it would not continue to do so.

Still, it felt strange to not be at work on a weekday. She felt badly that Zach and Chase were not at their worksite but here watching over her instead. At least Jackson had been able to go to work today. He woke up earlier than all of them and left for the fire station before dawn, leaving a note that he would be back in twenty-four hours. She supposed that she needed to get used to her "new normal." This was going to be her life until they caught Danny. Jillian's life, too. She smiled as Jillian flipped French toast onto a plate. Jillian was an awesome cook and was certainly in her element in the guys' state-of-the-art art kitchen.

"You need to eat something, Cass." Jillian had a determined look in her eye.

"I am not arguing with you. It smells yummy, and not eating isn't going to get Danny caught and sent back to prison any faster."

"Not in the mood to argue, huh? Interesting."

"I don't need to argue with you, Jillie. I have the men to argue with now." Cassie smirked.

"Yes, I imagine that all three of you have some pretty interesting arguments. Oh, my phone!" Jillian's phone was playing that catchy eighties tune again, and she ran to answer it. "Mark! What are you doing calling so early?"

From Jillian's tone, Cassie could tell that she was trying to find out how much Mark knew. Was Danny breaking out of prison enough to make the Chicago news?

"You heard? It's all over the news up there? Well, isn't that fan-fucking-tastic. Cassie will be thrilled to hear that Danny is getting even more attention for his antics. No, she and I are both fine. We're being guarded at Zach and Chase's home. I swear that we're safe. These guys and the sheriff aren't going to let anything happen to us, I promise."

Jillian handed the phone out to Cassie as Becca walked into the kitchen with Chase, Zach, and Ryan.

"He wants to talk to you."

"Just put him on speaker phone, Jill. If he wants to yell at me for putting you in danger then it shouldn't be a secret. Hi, Mark. You mad at me, sweetie?"

"Hell no! I'm worried about you. You and Jillian. This Trent guy is a loony tune, and there is no telling what he will do this time." Cassie could hear the worry and concern in Mark's voice.

"Mark? This is Sheriff Ryan Parks. I can assure you that we are keeping these ladies safe. They are being guarded twenty-four hours a day until Trent is caught. The entire town is on high alert looking for this guy."

"Jillian, do you want me to come down there? I can move some of my surgeries and get another doctor to cover for me. They owe me some favors. I can be there before the end of the day." Cassie heard Mark talking to someone in the background. "Travis says he can come down, too, sweetheart. We can help guard you girls and make sure you are safe. We'll catch the first plane to Florida."

"No! No, no, no. You are not coming down here to rescue me, Mark. Believe me, the men in this town are more than capable, and the sheriff is a real badass." Jillian gave Ryan a sidelong look. "Nothing is going to happen to us. We'll see you at Thanksgiving just as we planned and not a day earlier, brother."

Cassie thought she could actually see the sheriff's chest puff up a little as Jillian described him as a "badass."

"Okay, sweetie. But if you need us, don't hesitate to call. We can be there in hours. In the meantime, call me regularly so Trav and I don't worry, okay? Can we set a schedule of eight in the morning and evening?"

"Okay, okay. I will check in regularly. Ummm...Mark? I am afraid to ask, but does Mom know?"

"You lead a charmed life, little sister. Mom is visiting a friend in Indianapolis and is blissfully unaware that her wayward daughter is in any danger. Let's hope she stays unaware."

Cassie could see Jillian relaxing visibly. Her relationship with her mother could only be described as complicated. "Hey? Is that cutie who was dressed as a nurse there by any chance? Travis and I thought she was gorgeous."

All eyes turned to Becca, who had turned a bright shade of tomato red.

"Yes, she is bro. You want to talk to her?" Jillian was laughing so hard she had trouble answering.

"Nope. Just wondering. Call me at eight tonight, okay?"

"Okay, Mark. Talk to you then."

* * * *

Three days later, Jillian wanted to scream with boredom. Sheriff Ryan's estimate of Danny Trent showing up within sixteen hours turned out to be optimistic. Danny had yet to make an appearance, at least where anyone might have seen him. It was as if he had disappeared into thin air. But she knew better. She knew that Danny was out there somewhere just waiting for the right moment. She had only met Danny once. That night when he had come to pick up Cassie on their one and only date. He had looked at her as if he hated her. Jillian had known at that moment that something was wrong with him. He had wanted Cassie all to himself, not sharing any part with anyone.

"You look lost in thought, Jill."

Jillian looked up from staring out the window to Ryan. He really was a handsome man with broad shoulders and square jaw, looking yummy in his blue uniform. He wasn't as classically beautiful as Jackson, but Ryan had a raw masculinity that got to her every time she saw him. She hadn't been kidding when she had described him to Mark as a badass.

"I am so freakin' bored. Maybe Danny got hit by a truck and isn't going to make it here."

Ryan smiled at Jillian's attempt at humor as he sat down on the couch next to her. "We can only hope. But until we know for sure, we are keeping you and Cassie safe. A desperate man will do desperate things. There is no telling what he might do to Cassie, or you, for that matter."

"He never tried anything with me before, Ryan. And both Cassie and I know how to take care of ourselves."

Ryan sighed heavily. She really had given him a hard time the last few days, but he had never lost his patience with her.

"I can't take that chance, honey. With you and Cassie safe, I don't have to worry about you and can concentrate on finding Trent." He put his arm around her and pulled her close. She didn't fight him as she would have a few days ago. She wanted—hell, needed—the comfort.

He rubbed his chin on the top of her head. "When this is all over, the three of us are going to have a talk about our relationship. Let's get everything out in the open. I heard from Becca that you don't do relationships, but honestly, honey, you don't seem like a scaredy-cat to me."

She could hear the smile in his voice. He really deserved the truth. There wasn't any reason to wait to tell him. "I have avoided relationships in the past. My parents had a marriage from hell that was no example of how to be with another human being. But I'm moving past that. I'm not near as scared as I was a few years ago. But the real reason I'm staying away from you and Jackson is simple." Jillian sat up so she could look Ryan in the eye.

Ryan arched an eyebrow and rubbed his chin. "And that reason is?"

Jillian looked at Ryan calmly. "You're a Dom, Ryan. Jackson, too."

She started laughing at the shocked look on Ryan's face. "I guess you didn't know that I knew, huh?"

Ryan dragged his fingers through his brown-blond hair and scowled. Before he could get a word in, Jillian went on. "One of your former girlfriends told me. She said I should know what I was getting into. Although, she was clear that she didn't mind it and was a more-than-willing participant. She just thought I should know ahead of time. Were you planning on telling me or just springing it on me one night?"

Ryan's lips tightened, and she could tell he was not happy. Well, tough. He had wanted to talk about their relationship. Now they were.

"No, we were not planning on springing it on you. There was no point in bringing it up until we had been out on a few dates and seen if we were all compatible. Then, we would have slowly brought it into the relationship to see if you were comfortable with it. Nothing ever would have happened without your consent. Jack and I believe in Safe, Sane, and Consensual. I suppose you think we are a couple of sickos, huh?"

Jillian could see that Ryan's features were tense as he waited for her answer. He was a strong man, but she knew that a rejection from her because of this would hurt him. She didn't want that. He was a really nice man.

"No, I don't think you are sick at all. The fact is, I have a very open mind. My brother and his husband have played at this a little. I just don't think it's for me. I don't think I am submissive at all. You would be disappointed, Ryan. I can't be your slave twenty-four-seven."

Ryan barked in laughter. "First of all, I don't do twenty-four-seven. I'm only in charge in the bedroom. You can be in charge everywhere else. Secondly, how do you know you are not submissive? I can see the signs, honey. The way you drop your eyes when I use a certain tone of voice, the way your breathing quickens and your pulse beats harder when I give an order and it's not even to you."

Ryan lifted her chin with a finger so that she stared into his beautiful, hazel eyes that were hot with lust. "It takes a really strong woman to submit. Weak women need not apply. It's in submission that a strong woman, with a man she trusts, can truly be free. I never took you for a coward, Jillian. Before you reject Jackson and me, why don't you give us a chance? If you decide you're not submissive at all, well, Jack and I can have, and enjoy, vanilla sex just as much as the next guy. But don't you think you owe it to yourself to explore this opportunity? Believe me when I tell you that you will find out things about yourself you never knew."

Jillian's heart was pounding as she listened to Ryan talk about submission and freedom. She looked away from those eyes that saw too much. How had he noticed all that?

"It's a Dom's job to notice a sub's reactions, her emotions." Jillian looked at him in amazement. "No, I don't read minds, but all your thoughts are written on your face. Don't take up professional poker, honey." Ryan's tone was gentle and teasing.

"I am not making any decisions today, Sheriff. But I do see through your not-so-subtle double-dog dare that you threw out there. I stopped taking dares in elementary school."

Ryan grinned. "Fair enough. But once this is all over, Jackson and I are coming for you. Be warned."

* * * *

"We want to eat out, Zach."

Zach sighed in frustration at Cassie's hard tone. He tried to keep his own tone even and patient, despite his own frustration that had been building the last forty-eight hours.

"I know you do. But it is easier to protect you when we are inside the house."

"Jillian and I have been stuck in this house for days, barely allowed to go outside. We just want to go into town for some pizza. What could happen with all those people around? Danny never bothered me when others were around."

Zach could tell by the tight lines around Cassie's mouth that she was in a mood and not a happy camper. He didn't blame her, really. He was going crazy, too, and he had been allowed out of the house a few times in the last couple of days. He didn't have a chance to reply before Jillian started in.

"Yeah, we want out of here for a few hours. This is making us crazy. I bet Ryan would let us go."

"What would I let you do?" Sheriff Ryan must have heard his name from the kitchen and came to see what was going on.

Jillian stood up and poked the sheriff in the chest. "We want to go into town for pizza. We have had it."

The men exchanged a look that didn't bode well for them getting out of the house. "No can do, Jill. Listen, we just need to be patient a little longer. Trent will surface soon, and then this will be all over."

Cassie and Jillian both rolled their eyes. Cassie noticed Jillian looked ready to explode at the sheriff. She caught Cassie's eye with an evil grin. Cassie knew that look and always had a healthy fear of it. Jillian was up to no good.

"Well, if you think it is best, Sheriff." Jillian appeared to be giving in gracefully but just as quick grabbed a pillow from the couch and knocked the Sheriff right across the face. The Sheriff looked shocked, his brown-blond hair askew. Before he could recover, Jillian threw a pillow to Cassie and smashed him in the head again. The sheriff blinked the shock away, and his eyes narrowed as he gave his own version of an evil grin.

"So, that's how this is going to be? You know, I could have you arrested for assaulting an officer. But I think I will just make you pay myself." And with that, he grabbed his own cushion from a chair and gave Jillian a gentle swipe. "You better defend yourself, Zach. These women are armed and dangerous." Zach laughed and grabbed a pillow, too.

Jillian and Cassie flanked the couch in a zone defense. "I can't believe he hit a girl, Cassie!"

The battle was on.

They spent the next several minutes running around the living room taking swipes at each other. The women hitting the men as hard as they could, and the men taking it easier. They seemed to understand that Cassie and Jillian needed desperately to blow off steam. Ryan cornered Jillian as she ran behind the leather recliner. She feinted left, but he was on to her, and Cassie laughed as Ryan finally grabbed Jillian around the waist and threw her over his massive shoulder. He was so strong, he held her easily as he turned to Cassie.

"I have a hostage, and I will let her go if you both concede defeat and admit that Zach and I are superior in every way."

"Fuck you, Ryan! Don't say it, Cassie! These Neanderthals don't get to win!" Jillian's voice was a little breathless from running around and being hung upside down. Although she did have an excellent view of the sheriff's very fine ass. Cassie noticed that Jillian didn't seem to be struggling all that much.

The sheriff gave Jillian a swat on the ass. "Hush, now. Hostages don't get to talk, let alone curse."

Cassie giggled as a string of expletives came from somewhere near Ryan's ass. Jillian may not be struggling, but she was pissed.

Ryan just gave Jillian a few more swats as he held her easily. "What is it going to be, Cassie? I can spank her all night. Are you ready to concede?"

"Well, Sheriff, if she hangs upside down much longer, her head will explode. So, yes, we concede defeat."

"No, Cassie!" Jillian started to protest but only earned herself another smack on the ass from the sheriff. Cassie could have sworn she saw Jillian wriggle in excitement, but she must have been mistaken.

"Good. And Zach and I are superior in every way."

Cassie smirked. "And you and Zach are superior in some ways."

This time Zach came up behind Cassie and gave her a smack on the fanny. "In every way, Cass."

"Ouch! All right, you and Ryan are superior in every way."

"And devilishly sexy, too."

"Don't push me, Zach. You have to sleep sometime you know."

Zach laughed as he pulled her into his arms. She snuggled into his warmth. "You have no idea how much you scare me, angel."

Chapter 15

Chase gently nudged Cassie's shoulder, trying to wake her. He and Zach had a surprise for her that they hoped she liked. But she was a stubborn little thing and was refusing to wake up.

"C'mon, sweetheart. Wake up for us. Open those big, blue eyes." Chase shook her shoulder a little more. He smiled as one blue eye opened just a little, peered at the clock radio, then closed again. It was two in the morning.

"If you woke me up for sex, Chase, you are going to be disappointed. It is the middle of the freakin' night. Go away and let me sleep." She pulled the covers back up to her neck and tried to snuggle back to sleep.

Chase pulled the covers back down and lifted her out of the bed toward the bathroom. "Sorry, darlin'. But it is, in fact, time to wake up. And it is true I am disappointed we don't have time for a little nookie before we leave, but you need to get showered so we can get on the road before dawn."

That woke Cassie up a little. *Leave? On the road?* She opened her eyes to see Zach packing a bag for her as Chase carried her into the bathroom and set her down on the toilet.

"Ah, she wakes. You must be wondering where we are going." Chase pulled his old T-shirt that she had worn to bed up and over her head and lifted her into the shower.

"Wait!" Cassie held up her hand before Chase could turn on the water. "Wait, Chase. What is going on? Why is Zach packing me a bag? Has something happened?"

Zach walked into the bathroom and gave Cassie a big grin. "Have you told her yet, Chase?"

"Just about to, bro. Cassie, our love, we know that you and Jillian have been going crazy stuck in this house. So all four of us put our heads together and have decided that you have earned a little R & R. Somewhere we think you will be safe and still have fun. So shower up, sweetheart. Motorcade leaves as soon as you and Jillian are ready."

Cassie looked at them in a daze. She still hadn't woken up all the way yet. "Hold on. Where are we going?"

Chase smirked. "It's a surprise, love. It wouldn't be fun if it wasn't a surprise. But we think you are going to have fun and relax a little, okay? Trust us?"

Cassie sighed as she reached down for the faucet. "I have so far, haven't I? And look where it got me. Naked at two in the morning."

Chase and Zach's laughter trailed after them as they headed out the door.

"We'll go make coffee. Hurry up."

* * * *

Cassie shifted in the seat of the SUV to get a better view. They had hit the road by three in the morning, and the darkness kept her from getting a good view as to where they were going. She didn't know Florida all that well, so she probably wouldn't have been able to tell even if it had been light outside. Jillian rode in the truck with Jackson following right behind them, and she didn't have any more of a clue where they were going than Cassie did. She felt a little sad as she had felt Jillian's disappointment when the sheriff had told her he was not making the trip.

"I'm going to stay here and catch the bad guy, darlin'. But Jackson took a few days off work and will be making the trip with you. You guys have fun, and make sure you check in with me regularly." Then the sheriff had given Jillian a very tender kiss on the lips that appeared to take her breath away. The sheriff was sneaky. He was getting Jillian on his side a little at a time. Jillian really didn't stand a chance.

"Look up, Cassie. We're almost there!" Chase pointed out the window, and Cassie looked in confusion. They hadn't seen anything in the almost hour-long drive that gave any clue where they were headed.

"It's an electrical pole, Chase."

"Look closer. What is that electrical pole shaped like?"

Cassie harrumphed with impatience. She hadn't had a lot of sleep. Then she saw it.

"It's Mickey! It's shaped liked Mickey Mouse. We're going to Disney?" Cassie began to bounce up and down on the seat. She had never been to Disney before, and her guys must have remembered her mentioning it.

Chase turned from the passenger seat and gave her a big grin.

"Yes, we're going to Disney. We know you have never been. When you and Jillian assault an officer of the law with home decor, it is clear that the two of you need to blow off some steam. What better place than Disney? Disney is a pretty safe place. They require ID to get into the resort areas and chances are slim that Trent would show up at the parks with all the security that Disney has, especially since 9/11. The three of us can keep you safe and let you relax for a few days. So after you and Jillian fell asleep last night, we called Disney and made reservations. We wanted to leave in the middle of the night just in case, though. That's why you got the incredibly early wakeup call and the road trip in the dark."

"If I wasn't trapped in this seatbelt, I would hug both of you! This is a wonderful surprise. I can't believe the four of you cooked this up."

Cassie felt such love for them at that moment. They had really recognized how stressed she was hanging around the house all day and had made it their business to take care of her. It made her love and trust them even more, if it were possible. She smiled and put a hand on each of their shoulders.

"I love you both so much. More every day. And I can't wait to show my appreciation."

Zach laughed from the driver's seat. "We already have plans as to how you can show that appreciation. Be prepared."

* * * *

They called Ryan to let him know they had arrived safely. He said that there was nothing new to report there either and to enjoy themselves. They decided to visit the Magic Kingdom first. Cassie couldn't believe that the monorail ran right through the hotel. It was a quick and smooth ride to the park where the boys made sure they had fun all day long. A weekday in early November was apparently a good time to visit the parks as the crowds weren't too bad, and they waited in very few lines.

Now they were relaxing in the steakhouse of the Contemporary enjoying a great meal and an equally wonderful view of the park. Even Jillian had mellowed enough to allow Jackson to put his arm around her and steal a kiss or two. Cassie was in her favorite place— between her two men. Zach was making lazy circles on her lower back with his warm hands while Chase made her giggle by tickling her nose with the ends of her long hair.

At first, Cassie had been self-conscious to be with two men outside of Plenty, but no one seemed to pay any attention or notice. If they did, they were too polite to mention anything. She slowly sipped her glass of Merlot as the fireworks show lit up the sky brightly. It was beautiful, but what she really wanted was some alone time with Zach and Chase.

Cassie set her wine glass down and ran her hand up Zach's thigh and her other hand trailed down Chase's broad chest. Zach's head swiveled from the fireworks display, and she found herself looking up into his blue-topaz eyes. A dimple creased his cheek as he smiled down at her.

"What are you up to, angel?" His larger hand trapped her smaller one at the top of his hard muscled thigh.

"I believe someone said something about showing my appreciation and to prepare myself. I believe I am fully prepared to show both of you how much I appreciate you." Cassie batted her eyelashes at him and fantasized about running her tongue in those dimples. Zach loved when she did that. She felt Chase entwine his fingers in her hair at the scalp and gently, but firmly, pull her head back so he could kiss her. When he was done, she was breathless, her lips tingly, and her panties soaked. She would never get over how these men affected her.

"Ah, so responsive, sweetheart," Chase said lightly against her lips. "I think it is time to take you upstairs. We have some ideas as to how you can show your appreciation."

Cassie heard Jackson's groan from across the table. "Get a room, you three. Jillian and I don't want to see you guys making out. I'm guessing the other diners don't either, but I could be wrong there."

"I think we'll retire for the evening if you don't mind, Jack. You can take care of Jillian?" Zach stood and helped Cassie up while Chase signed the check.

"Of course, I can take care of Jillian. We are going to finish our wine and then get some sleep, too. It has been a long day, buddy." As if on cue, Jillian gave a big yawn and laid her head on Jackson's shoulder. Cassie noticed how protectively Jackson held her. His gaze was almost worshipful in its intensity.

"It has been a long day. You three go on. Jack can take me back to the room in a few minutes. We'll be fine."

Chase wrapped his arm around her and whispered in her ear, "Let's get upstairs. Zach and I can't wait to get you alone."

* * * *

Zach's hands slid down her arms and around her waist as he pressed his lips to her neck just at the spot where it met her shoulder. He pulled her against him, and she could feel his impressive erection pressing against her lower back. Chase crowded her in front, and she tipped her head up to give him better access to her lips. She felt him nip at her lower lip then run his tongue in a soothing motion over the love bite. She tried to open her mouth to suck his tongue inside, but he kept pulling away, nibbling at her lips, chin, and earlobes, and then running his tongue over them, again and again, until she was crazy with wanting him to kiss her deeply. He was always such a tease.

"Ready to show some appreciation?" Chase spoke softly into the shell of Cassie's ear.

"I'm trying, but you're making it difficult." Cassie tried again unsuccessfully to capture his lips with hers. She felt Zach's hands skim down her sides to rest on her hips. She heard Chase's soft chuckle in her ear.

"Let's get these clothes off of you before Zach here goes all caveman and tells you to strip."

Cassie felt Chase and Zach's hands working on the buttons of her dress. They lifted it over her head and then tossed it aside. Her panties were next, and she watched as Chase tossed them over his shoulder. Their hands seemed to be everywhere at once, touching, stroking, and caressing.

Chase's fingers brushed over her nipples, and she could feel them tighten in response. His head dipped, and he licked at one tight bud while caressing the other. The sensation went straight to her clit, and she felt her arousal tighten in her abdomen. Zach's fingers dipped into her already slippery cunt. His fingers left a trail of heat wherever they touched and teased. Her clit swelled to attention and begged Zach's talented fingers to caress it. She heard herself moan and caught her breath as Zach's fingers starting circling her clit at the same time Chase sucked her nipple hard and pinched the other.

"Please let me come!" Her voice sounded breathless and tortured to her ears.

"Yes, Cassie. Come for us now." As always, Zach's dark and commanding tone sent Cassie over.

Multicolored lights flashed in front of Cassie's eyes, and her body tensed with pleasure. It started in her pussy, and the fire spread to her nipples and down her legs. Her knees gave out, and she would have fallen if Zach and Chase hadn't been holding her so firmly. She felt herself being lifted and gently placed on the bed.

She watched as her men quickly stripped out of their clothes, revealing their hard, muscled bodies. Their hard cocks jutted out from their bodies deliciously. She reached out and ran her hands lightly up and down their throbbing shafts, drawing groans from each of them.

She leaned forward and let her tongue drag along Zach's velvety shaft and then repeated the process on Chase's hard cock. Her pussy dripped honey at the thought of those cocks filling her full, pumping into her hard. Zach's fingers tangled in her hair, and Chase's fingertips caressed her cheek. She turned back to Zach and drew him into her mouth as far as she could. She felt him bump the back of her throat. Her other hand pumped Chase's cock using the pre-cum to lubricate her way. She pulled off Zach's cock with a pop and quickly engulfed Chase's cock in her warm mouth. She sucked and licked his cock while stroking Zach. Sometimes having two cocks to pleasure was a lot of work. She wanted to make sure that each of them never got neglected. They certainly never neglected her.

* * * *

Chase groaned as Cassie's hot mouth moved up and down his cock. Her tongue swirled over the head on each out stroke, and he could feel his balls tighten as his orgasm neared. He reluctantly pulled her off his cock and stepped back to diminish the temptation to fuck her warm, wet mouth and shoot his seed down her throat. His own throat tightened a little with emotion, and he looked down at the woman he and his brother loved more than they ever imagined they could love someone. He would protect her with his life and spend that life doing everything he could to make her happy.

He looked at Zach and saw his expression reflected there.

"We want to come inside you, Cassie. Move over on the bed. It's time to show your appreciation. We have plans for you tonight." Chase nudged her and lay down on his back, stretching his long legs to the end of the bed.

Zach smirked at him as he guided Cassie into place. Chase felt her soft skin brush his as she straddled his thighs. He ran his hands up the silky skin of her back, tugging her down against his chest. His cock hardened painfully as her dripping pussy cuddled against him. He blew out a breath as he tried to get control of his arousal. He and Zach had plans tonight, and he needed to hold back until it was time. He reached for the condom and handed it to Cassie. She gave him a brilliant and evil smile. He watched as she tore open the condom with her teeth and proceeded to torture him by rolling the condom on him slowly while caressing his balls, rolling them between her small fingers.

"Ride Chase, Cassie. Show him some love."

Cassie began to lower herself slowly onto his dick, and his mind short-circuited a little bit as each inch of him was enfolded into her hot, wet pussy. It hugged him tightly and felt like wet velvet. Cassie lowered herself up and down, her head thrown back and eyes closed with pleasure.

* * * *

Cassie fucked herself up and down on Chase. She could feel every ridge of his huge cock against her pussy walls stretching her to accommodate him. She felt Zach's hands on her back pushing her down onto Chase's chest.

"Hold still on Chase, Cassie. Tonight, we take you together. I am going to fuck this pretty ass while Chase fucks that tight, wet pussy."

She felt Zach's hands caressing the globes of her ass and then running his fingers down the crease. His fingers sent tingles up and down her spine, making her want to ride Chase hard as arousal dripped from her pussy. They had been patiently stretching her with their fingers and the plugs for weeks. Her excitement hitched up several notches at the thought of them taking her together finally. She jumped a little at the cold lubricant dripping between her cheeks and running down her crack.

"Easy, angel. We are going to take this slow and easy. Relax on Chase and breathe in and out. This is going to take a while." Zach stroked down her spine soothingly as he spoke softly to her.

She tried to force herself to relax under his strong but gentle hands. Chase took her face between his hands and began to kiss her gently at first and then more demandingly, sweeping his tongue in and out of her mouth. She felt Zach massaging her ass and then his finger probing her back hole, pressing for entry. She felt pressure and then a burn as her muscle gave way to the intrusion. As quickly as the burn receded, the pleasure started. He moved his finger in and out, adding a second finger and the second burn as her muscle stretched further. He scissored his fingers, stretching her, before adding a third.

"Good girl, angel. Keep relaxed, and this will be easier. You are so hot and tight. I can't wait to fuck you here. How does it feel, angel?" Zach's voice sounded tight and harsh as if he kept a tight rein on his emotions.

"I feel so full, and so—" Cassie couldn't find the words.

Zach tried to supply them. "Submissive, Cassie? Do you feel submissive to Chase and me?" His fingers fucked her ass in and out, in and out, as he pressed her down onto Chase's chest.

"Oh, oh, yes! I feel full and submissive, Zach." She panted as her pleasure climbed higher with every pump of his fingers. Her body truly did feel submissive to these men who had mastered her with pleasure. She had never thought of herself as submissive, but she trusted these men with her body and her life. They protected her and pleasured her unselfishly.

Another frisson of pleasure ran up her spine and down to her clit as he continued to fuck and stretch her back hole, moving her closer and closer to an orgasm. Suddenly, his fingers were gone, and her cry of loss was muffled by Chase's mouth. Despite having Chase's enormous cock in her pussy, she felt empty and squirmed back to find Zach's fingers, needing something in her ass to bring her to release. Surprisingly, it was Chase who gave her a sharp smack on her bottom and held her tight so she couldn't move.

"Shhh, Cassie. I am going to give you what you want. Just be patient." Zach petted her ass a few times, and she felt the blunt head of his cock lined up to her ass. Another dousing of lubricant ran down her crack, and he pushed the head of his cock relentlessly into her back hole. The stretching from the plugs previously and his fingers tonight had done their job, and her muscles gave way quickly. His hands clenched her hips and held her still as he began to make little movements, pushing farther into her each time.

Time seemed to stand still and a fine sheen of sweat covered their bodies as he gently but firmly pushed into her tight hole over and over again. Finally, he was fully seated, and she heard his ragged breathing. Cassie was fully impaled on both her men. She knew it was by sheer will that he held still waiting for a sign from her that it was okay to move. The pleasure of being so full of cock was overwhelming, and she was on the edge of release almost immediately. She pushed back against Zach and then forward to Chase to get them moving. She needed to come badly.

"Christ, Chase. She is so fucking tight back here. There is no way I will last long. Get moving, bro." Zach's voice sounded strained in a way she had never heard before.

She soaked in the power and pleasure of affecting her men so strongly. She could please and pleasure both her men now at the same time. More lubricant was poured down her ass crack as Zach and Chase each started moving, slowly at first, then picking up speed. Zach pulled out and Chase slammed in hard, then Chase pulled out and Zach pounded her ass. Over and over, time after time, until she was overcome with the feeling of their cocks moving in and out of her and the pleasure that started in her pussy was pushing out over her whole body. She trembled on the brink of release, waiting for Zach's permission before allowing herself to climax. He didn't make her wait long.

"Come! Come now!" Zach's voice in hear ear sounded like it was dragged over gravel.

Her body recognized his permission and released the tension and pleasure that had been building in a ball of white lightning. Her pussy clamped down on Chase's cock, and she could feel her vise grip on Zach. Bright, white lights flashed in front of her eyes, and she went blind for a moment as wave after wave of pleasure ran from her eyes to her toes, shaking her slight body and throwing her back against Zach.

She was just coming down when Chase's fingers caressed her clit and it sent her over again, those waves almost painful in their pleasure. She heard herself scream their names as they groaned their own releases. She felt their bodies stiffen and bow, then relax.

They petted and stroked her as she slowly came down from the most intense pleasure she had ever known. Having both her men fuck her at the same time had given her the kind of grab-you-by-the-throat-and-shake-you-around orgasm she had never known existed.

She collapsed, exhausted, on top of Chase, and Zach leaned over her. Their bodies were sweaty from their lovemaking and sticky from her juices which had gushed from her as she climaxed. Their breathing slowed, and her quivering lessened. She felt Zach moving, and he carefully pulled out of her even as she mourned the loss.

"I need to take care of the condom, honey. Just relax, and we will take care of you." Zach disappeared into the bathroom and came out a few minutes later with a washcloth. Chase then lifted her, and Zach finished the job of moving her aside so Chase could also take care of his condom. Zach gently cleaned her up with the warm cloth, and she tried to protest the intimacy.

"Little late to be shy, Cassie. I've spanked this ass, fucked this ass, and fucked this pussy and mouth, too. Cleaning you up afterward doesn't seem like a big deal after that. You belong to us, and we take care of our woman." Zach chuckled as she blushed. He cleaned the honey from her thighs and disappeared into the bathroom again to put the washcloth in the hamper. Chase and Zach each took a side of the bed and cuddled her front and back.

"I don't know about you, Zach, but I sure feel really appreciated." Chase smirked as he kissed the back of her neck.

"I do, too, bro. In fact, I don't think I have ever felt so *appreciated* in my life." Zach laughed and hugged Cassie closer. She snuggled closer to her men. She felt like they truly belonged to each other now. She loved them more than anything, and she felt wrapped in their love for her, and for the first time in several days, she felt safe.

Chapter 16

Danny pulled into the service station and tugged his baseball cap low on his forehead. You never know if the cameras in these places work or not, he thought. But just in case, he would keep his hat low and his head down. He needed to fill up the tank and add water to the radiator. The piece-of-shit car he had stolen turned out to be almost more trouble than it was worth. It kept overheating, which necessitated Danny adding water to the radiator every time he stopped for gas.

As he pumped gas into the beater, he looked around for any cops. He hadn't seen one cop for the entire trip from Illinois, and it seemed too good to be true. So far he had only traveled at night. Yesterday, he had found a deserted parking lot and slept in the car. Now he was in Georgia, so he wanted to press on through and get to Cassandra. He knew that the cops would be looking for him in that little town she had moved to, so he needed to set up base outside of town. He wouldn't be stupid enough to just charge in and try and see her. He would watch and bide his time. Cassandra wasn't going anywhere. She would be waiting for him when he got there, and they would be reunited forever.

* * * *

It sucked to be home. If things had been normal, it would have been fine to come home from Disney. But Danny still had not been caught, let alone spotted, so they were back on lockdown. The trip to Disney had been wonderful, and she had enjoyed two wonderful days and nights with Zach and Chase. But now they were stuck in the house all the time just waiting for something to happen. And to top it all off, Jillian had apparently picked up a nasty bug while at Disney and was miserable. Zach was going to take Jillian to the doctor today and get her checked for strep throat.

"Zach, will you and Jillian pick up milk on the way back from the doctor?"

"Sure will, Cass. We'll probably need to stop anyway if we need to fill a prescription for Jillian. She also says she wants popsicles for her throat."

Cassie ran her hands up Zach's chest and linked them behind his neck, tugging him down for a kiss. Zach's hands splayed across her bottom, pulling her closer to his hard cock. His tongue ran along her bottom lip before giving it a little nip.

"Stop tempting me, angel. Jillian's appointment is at five o'clock, the last one of the day, so we don't have time for what my cock has in mind. But later, I'll take you up on that offer."

Jillian walked into the kitchen looking absolutely miserable. Her complexion was pale, and her nose was bright red. Her eyes looked watery, and she was carrying a box of tissues.

"Is it time to go yet? I don't want to miss my appointment. I was lucky to get in to see Dr. Steve. Man, this town needs more doctors." Before Jillian could say anything else, she went into a sneezing fit that left her leaning against a chair.

"Yeah, we should get going. It looks like it's going to storm out there, too, so grab an umbrella. Cassie, be sure to stay in the house with Chase. I'll have my cell if you need me."

"I know the rules. I won't leave. But I almost wish that I had a cold so I could go into town and get out of this house."

Jillian sneezed a few more times and blew her nose.

"Trust me, Cassie. You don't want this cold. I'm miserable."

Cassie nodded sympathetically. Jillian really did look miserable, and getting out of the house really wasn't worth it.

* * * *

Thunder rumbled, and a flash of lightning made Chase look up from his laptop and out the window. The sky was an ominous charcoal, and it looked like they were in for the kind of rainstorm that Florida was famous for. He glanced at his watch and hoped that Zach and Jillian were on their way back. It hadn't rained in a while, and the roads would be dangerous. Non-Floridians didn't realize that a wet Florida road could be as slick as ice if it hadn't rained for several days. Luckily, Zach had grown up here and knew to be careful until the rain had washed away the oil rising from the road. More lightning and louder thunder shook the house, and Cassie came running into the office and jumped on his lap with a laugh.

"Hey! Careful where you land, babe. I got something there that you seem to like. Be gentle." He gave Cassie a squeeze and adjusted her on his lap so she was draped over his knees and he was looking down into her pretty, blue eyes.

"Scared? It's just a storm, sweetheart. You need to get used to these if you are going to live in Florida."

"Not too scared, but this seemed like a good time to come in here and get some sugar from my guy." Cassie closed her eyes and pursed her lips as if waiting for a kiss from her Prince Charming. Well, hell, he could be charming, too.

He leaned over and gently brushed her lips with his again and again until her lips gently parted. His tongue slid sensuously between her soft lips and explored each part of her mouth. He knew Cassie liked having the roof of her mouth tickled, and when he did, he was rewarded with her muffled moan. He cradled her in his arms as he stood to head toward the bedroom only tearing his lips from hers so he wouldn't run into any walls.

A boom of thunder and a flash of lightning made them both jump.

"Shit, that sounded close." Cassie cuddled closer to Chase. She wasn't afraid of thunderstorms, but she wasn't too fond of them either.

"Yeah, sounds like it is right on top of us. I hope Zach and Jillian aren't caught in this. It's a downpour out there." Chase carried Cassie over to the window where he could see that it was practically raining sideways. Lightning flashed every few seconds, and thunder rumbled so loudly, the house vibrated.

Another loud boom and a crack and Chase saw the lights start to flicker. It wasn't unusual for them to lose power in a bad storm. They had lots of trees in this area, and broken limbs took down power lines on occasion. Luckily, they had installed the generator when building the house.

"I think we might lose power, sweetheart. Don't worry..."

Before Chase could even finish reassuring Cassie, the power flickered one last time and then was out. Chase set Cassie down on the chair and scowled as he looked out the window.

"Looks like I am going to get soaked starting the generator." He had hoped that the power might come right back on, but as the time ticked away it was clear that wasn't going to happen. He felt Cassie's arms slide around his waist from behind.

"Well, I guess I will just have to strip those wet clothes off of you, Chase, and then use my body heat to warm you up." Chase heard Cassie giggle as her hand trailed down his abs to his already hard cock.

"Oooo, what do we have here?" Cassie cooed.

"One, hard, damn cock, babe. And it's all yours as soon as I go out and start the generator. You stay inside the house." He felt Cassie give his cock a few gentle strokes through his jeans before releasing him.

"Hurry, Chase. I have plans for that hard cock. I'll go wait in the bedroom, handsome."

Chase gave Cassie a nudge toward the bedroom as he grabbed a flashlight from the desk drawer and his key ring from the desktop.

Starting the generator wasn't hard, but he would get soaked. He grinned as he thought about how Cassie would strip him out of his wet clothes. He walked quickly through the dark house to the front door. The sooner he started the generator the sooner he could join Cassie in the bedroom.

He ducked out into the rain and ran around the side of the house. He was soaked instantly from the deluge of water sliding off the roof and the sound it made as it landed on the side patio competed with the rolling thunder above. Finding the right key on his key ring, he opened the metal box to turn the generator key, hearing it roar to life and seeing the lights go on in the house through the window, when he felt something poking into his ribs.

"Don't move, asshole. I will blow your fucking head off and not blink an eye. Turn around slow, and put your hands where I can see them."

Fuck. Fuck. Double Fuck. How had someone snuck up on me? Is Cassie okay?

Chase turned, and the gun at his ribs backed away. He raised his hands over his head and tried to keep calm. Chase narrowed his eyes against the torrential downpour as he tried to get a good look at the infamous Danny Trent. He knew it was Trent. It couldn't be anyone else. His brown hair was trimmed short, but his face was covered with several days of whiskers. Trent appeared to be in his early thirties and pretty boy handsome. A little under six feet tall and in pretty good shape with ill-fitting clothes that were soaked through. He held a gun pointed directly at Chase.

Keep him calm and distracted and, most importantly, away from Cassie.

"You must be Trent. We've been expecting you. What took you so long?" Chase backed up a few steps to make some room between him and the gun.

"Stop! Don't move, asshole. I'm in charge here, and you do exactly what I tell you and I might, just might, let you live." Even through the rain, Chase could see Trent glowering at him.

"You really had everyone looking for you, Trent. Where have you been all this time? How did you get away from the police?" *Keep him talking and calm until Zach shows up or I can figure a way to get Cassie out of here. I just hope Cassie doesn't come looking for me.*

The rain was slowing, and Chase could see Danny smirking at him as he pointed the gun at him.

"Cops are fucking stupid. I hid right under their fucking noses for days. Then I hid under your cops' noses for days, too. I've been waiting and watching for an opportunity like today. The other men and woman are gone, and you are here alone with Cassandra. Too bad for you, but good luck for me."

Chase used his calmest voice. The one he used with skittish or wild horses. "Let's talk about this, Trent."

* * * *

Cassie hid behind the corner of the house listening as Chase tried to reason with the nearest thing to evil that Cassie had ever known. Thank God she had come to look for Chase when the power came back on in the house but he hadn't returned. One look outside and she saw Danny with a gun pointed at Chase. She had quickly pressed the panic button on the alarm knowing that Ryan would be on his way. She just needed to keep Chase alive until the cavalry arrived. She knew that reasoning with Danny was a waste of time. He had lost the ability to reason years ago.

"Cassie's not even here, Trent. She went to the doctor with Jillian and Zach."

"Bullshit. I saw the others leave, and she wasn't with them. And her name is Cassandra."

"Okay, Trent, she's Cassandra. Let's talk this over, man. No way is this going to end well for you. Every cop in Plenty is out looking for you, and there is no way in hell I am going to let you leave with her. You won't get away."

Cassie held her breath as Danny stepped closer to Chase, waving the gun. "Fuck you. I am taking what belongs to me. I am tired of all this shit. Do you think I care if you live or die? I will kill you and anyone else who comes between me and Cassandra. Do you know how long I have waited for this, asshole? How many nights I lay awake in that fucking cell waiting for my one chance to be with her again. She's mine, dammit, and I am going to take her with me!"

Danny's voice sounded higher and slightly hysterical now. He had taken another step closer to Chase, and she knew she didn't have much time to do something. If Danny shot Chase at close range, Chase would die.

"I am not letting you take her, Trent. You are going to have to go through me, my brother, and everyone in this town to take her. If you hurt her, I will kill you, simple as that."

Shit. Why was Chase taunting him? She had to do something now.

"You won't get the chance. I am killing you now."

Cassie knew this was the moment, and she had to do something now. She saw Danny steady the gun and point right at Chase's heart. She lunged from behind the corner of the house screaming at the top of her lungs to get Danny's attention.

"Danny!"

Danny turned, throwing his aim off slightly as he pulled the trigger. She pushed Danny to the ground and landed on top of him. She tried to remember everything she and Jillian has been taught in the self-defense classes they had both taken in Chicago. She had to make sure Danny stayed down on the ground and then get the gun. She landed a punch to his solar plexus, knocking the wind out of him, but he came back at her with the butt of the gun and knocked her off him with a hard blow to her temple. She fell on her back and felt the trickle of blood running down her cheek. She could see Chase lying on the ground with a large blood stain on his chest.

God, Chase is dead. I was too late. Oh God, I can't lose him.

"Fucking cunt! You'll pay for that!"

Through her daze, Cassie could see Danny's face contorted with rage. He barely looked human as he raised the gun to point it straight at her.

"You'll die, and then I will die. We will be together for eternity, Cassandra. You belong to me."

Cassie didn't want Danny to be the last thing she saw in life. She turned her head to look at Chase on the ground but blinked when she didn't see him lying there.

What the—

Crack!

With a thud, Danny went down, and Chase stood behind him covered in his own blood, holding a small tree branch with a disgusted look on his face before he fell to his knees. It looked like Chase had hit Danny in the head.

"He called me an asshole. No one calls me an asshole." Chase dropped the branch, pressed his right hand over the blood stain on his left shoulder, and crawled to her side. "You okay, sweetheart? Are you hurt?" Chase's voice was urgent and gravelly.

"Me? You were shot, Chase! Are you okay? Let me see!" Cassie frantically tried to sit up and pull his hand away from the wound, but the world started spinning and she fell back on the wet grass.

"You took quite a shot to the head, babe, and I have lost a lot of blood. We need to get to the house, so we can phone for an ambulance. You need a doctor, Cassie." Cassie saw Chase was pale, and she knew that he was staying conscious for her. He must be in all kinds of pain with a bullet in his shoulder.

"I can get to the house, Chase. I really can. We can lean on each other. But the cops are probably on their way. I pushed the panic button before I came outside."

"Good girl, Cassie. You're pretty brave, sweetheart. Let's try and get into the house now. I don't want Danny coming to where he can get you."

Cassie saw Chase snag Danny's gun and then, using his good hand, pushed to his feet.

"Okay, sweetheart, you next. I'll try to help you." Chase reached with his good hand, but Cassie knew she would pull him down. He swayed on his feet and could barely stand himself. She got on all fours and eased her legs under her, pushing herself up despite the hammering in her skull and the wave of dizziness that engulfed her. Cassie leaned against Chase as he leaned against the side of the house, and they dragged themselves toward the front door. The sounds of speeding vehicles down their long driveway made them look up.

Cassie felt relief flood her body, and she slumped against the doorframe. It was Zach and Jillian in one truck and Ryan in another. The cavalry was here.

Chapter 17

Zach raced up the long drive feeling his tires slip on the wet pavement. His heart was racing, and Jillian looked terrified. He knew he needed to slow down, but he had to get to Cassie. Ryan had called him as he and Jillian were leaving the doctor and told him that the panic button had been tripped. He had tried to call the house, but there had been no answer. Now he and Jillian were driving like a bat out of hell to get to Chase and Cassie. He slid to a stop and saw a man lying in the yard at the side of the house. Zach panicked for a moment before realizing it wasn't Chase. Before he could stop her, Jillian jumped from the truck and ran to Cassie and Chase in the doorway of the house.

Christ! They are covered in blood!

Zach jumped from the truck and headed straight for them and could hear Ryan hot on his heels.

Chase was pale and slumped over but managed shakily, "We're okay. Cassie needs to see a doctor and someone needs to collect Trent from the side yard before he comes to."

"I radioed for an ambulance, man, and am heading to collect Trent now." Ryan disappeared out of the house, and Zach helped Chase sit down and lifted Cassie into his arms, stroking her back to soothe her. He could feel her trembling as the adrenaline drained from her body. Jillian disappeared into the kitchen and came out with a couple of dish towels. One had ice in it, and she handed that to him for Cassie. The other she placed on Chase's chest and held it there, trying to stem the flow of blood. He could see Jillian was pale, but she was obviously holding it together for Cassie.

Zach opened his mouth to ask what had happened but didn't have a chance before he heard a car start up and peel out of the driveway, fishtailing on the wet pavement. He saw Ryan heading for his truck to go after it.

"Jillian! Take care of them until the ambulance arrives. I am going after Trent!"

Zach handed Cassie to Jillian, ran to catch up with Ryan, and jumped into the passenger side of the truck before Ryan could pull away. Ryan had a lump on the side of his head that hadn't been there moments before.

"No fucking way, Zach. This is police business. No civilians. I can't be responsible for your safety." Ryan looked pissed, but Zach didn't care. Trent had hurt his brother and his woman. He wouldn't be left out of the capture.

"I can take care of myself, and you know it. We're wasting time, Ryan. Let's go after him."

Ryan sighed but quickly backed up the truck and raced up the driveway after Trent. His car turned left onto the main road and gathered speed. Zach could hear sirens in the distance and knew the ambulance was on its way for Chase and Cassie.

"I can't believe Trent is running. He knows he's been made. What is he thinking?" Ryan was pushing a hundred miles an hour and struggling to keep the truck on the slick roads. Zach didn't know what Trent was thinking either, but there was one thing he did know— Trent was a man with nothing to lose. He had learned in the military that there was nothing more dangerous than someone who had nothing left to lose.

"There's a spare gun in the glove compartment, Zach. I hope we don't have to use it, but I know you know your way around a firearm. If you have to shoot it, shoot to kill. He obviously isn't going to stay down. He should still be laid out in the side yard from where Chase put a hurt on him, but the motherfucker is determined to go out in a blaze of glory. The bastard hit me with a tree branch."

Zach could hear the determination in Ryan's voice. He knew that Ryan took the safety of Plenty seriously. Between the two of them, Trent was going to be in trouble.

It was hard to see anything as the sun had gone down, and Trent had turned away from the town toward the quarries. The only lights were the headlights from the cars as this far out of town there were no streetlights.

"Is that smoke coming from Trent's car?"

Zach squinted into the distance to where Ryan had pointed. It appeared that the engine on the old car that Trent was driving was overheating and sending billows of smoke into the air. With the lack of lighting in this area and the smoke pouring from the engine, Zach doubted Trent could see much. The road straightened out, and Trent began to pull away from them, obviously trying to use this to his advantage.

"He's getting away, Ryan, can't this truck go any faster?" There was no way he was going to let Trent get away if he had to wrestle the wheel from Ryan to do it.

"The curve in the road is coming up, and the roads are slicker than shit. It would be suicide to speed up any faster than we are already going. Shit! I just hope I can make the curve."

Zach realized they were close to the big lake at the quarry where the Halloween party had been held, and Trent was heading straight for it. A stranger in this area would never see the drop-off this time of night, and the smoke billowing out of his engine would make visibility even worse. He felt Ryan slowing down a little to make the turn. It looked like Trent sped up even faster, and before he knew what happened, Trent's taillights disappeared from sight. Ryan continued slowing down the truck and brought the vehicle to a halt. They both jumped out with guns at the ready. The chance of Trent surviving the twenty-plus-foot drop into the deep lake was remote, but he still couldn't believe the bastard had gotten up and walked away from their house, either.

They cautiously approached the edge of the drop and peered over. The back of the car was disappearing, sinking down into the deep water. Although every instinct told him that Trent was dead, Zach knew he couldn't live with himself if he didn't try to get him out of the car. He quickly toed off his shoes and jumped into the water. He was a Navy SEAL, a strong swimmer, and was trained for survival. If there was any chance Trent was alive, he would get him out of the car.

He closed off his mind and followed his years of training as he swam through the water, quickly locating the sinking car. Luckily, Trent hadn't locked the car, and Zach was able to pull the door open as the pressure equalized inside and outside. Trent was slumped over the wheel, and Zach pulled him from the car and headed straight for the surface. His lungs burned from the effort. He pulled Trent toward the bank of the lake, and Ryan was there to help him pull his body to dry land. Ryan placed his fingers on Trent's neck as Zach tried to catch his breath. Trent had been dead weight as he had pulled him up, and no bubbles had come from his nose.

"He's dead. His skull and his chest appear to have taken the brunt of the fall, probably crushed. Hitting the water from more than twenty feet up was like the car hitting solid cement. He was probably dead on impact, Zach. There isn't anything we can do for him now."

Zach could hear the approaching sirens as he struggled to his feet. There was nothing they could do for Trent, but he needed to see Cassie and Chase to make sure they were okay.

"Easy there, Zach. Catch your breath, man. I'll have one of my deputies drive you to the hospital to see Chase and Cassie. I need to stay here and deal with this. Will you check on Jillian for me? I'll come to the hospital when this is all cleared up."

Zach combed his fingers through his wet hair and let out a long breath. This long nightmare was really going to be over for Cassie now.

"Sure, Ry. One of us will call you and let you know how everyone is, okay?"

Zach stared down at the dead body of Danny Trent. In death, his face looked peaceful, almost innocent. It was hard to believe that, mere minutes ago, he was trying to kill his brother and his girlfriend. Zach had seen plenty of death when he had been a SEAL. He had never celebrated the death of his enemies, and he didn't do it tonight.

* * * *

Her head hurt like a bitch, and the hospital staff wouldn't let her see Chase. She had asked Jillian to stay with Chase when they had been separated at the hospital. Chase had held her hand in the back of the ambulance as the EMTs had hooked him to IVs and tried to stabilize him. He had managed to stay conscious for her until they gave him the pain medication. They wouldn't let her lose consciousness and kept asking her what her name was and who the president was. With her head pounding and her terror over Chase, it had been extremely annoying. Only Jillian's presence had kept her from snapping the heads off of the EMTs.

Jillian had kept saying, "They are trying to make sure you are okay. They are helping Chase."

When they arrived, Chase had been taken to surgery and she had been given a CT scan for her head. Now she lay in her hospital room, in pain and irritable. She hadn't seen Jillian in what seemed like forever, and fear over Chase's safety was sending her blood pressure ever higher. The nurses kept coming in and fussing over the pressure reading and threatening to sedate her if she didn't calm down. Cassie wanted to remain awake to hear about Chase and also what happened to Danny. She was worried for Zach and Ryan. She knew Danny was evil, and he would kill without remorse. She almost cried out in relief when Zach and Jillian walked into her room and came to her side immediately. She reached for Zach and hugged him tightly.

"Okay, angel. Everything is okay. I got you. Nothing is going to happen to you ever again. You're okay, and Chase is going to be okay, too." Zach stroked her back in a soothing motion. She could feel her tears of relief running down her face, but she didn't know how to stop them. She was really tired of crying.

"Is Chase really okay? Are you okay?" Her voice sounded shaky, and she felt Zach's hold tighten a little on her.

"Yes, I am fine and Chase is going to be fine. He is in surgery now, but Jillian talked to the doctor, and there is no reason he won't make a full recovery. He is going to be hell to live with, darlin'. He's going to want you to wait on him hand and foot. He likes to be spoiled that way." Zach's laugh rumbled in his chest, and she could feel it through the thin hospital gown. He felt warm and strong, and she breathed in the masculine scent that was his alone. He lifted his head, and his strong hands gently wiped the tears from her eyes.

"The question really is, how are you?"

Jillian laughed. "That one I can answer. The doctor says she has a mild concussion. They are going to keep her overnight for observation, and then she needs to take it easy for a few days. The hit on the head, however, did nothing for her personality as she has been terrorizing the EMTs and nurses alike for the last hour or so while I was getting word on Chase."

Cassie felt her face get warm. Had she been that bad?

"I'll make it up to them. When can I see Chase?" She tried to sit up and swing her legs out of the bed, and the room began to spin. Zach gently pressed her back into the pillows.

"Whoa! You are staying right where you are. Chase will be in surgery for a while longer then recovery. You can see him in the morning. The nurses are going to come in here and give you some pain medication to help you sleep. I'll stay here with you tonight. The nurses are going to bring in a cot for me. Jackson will take Jillian home, which is where we'll take you tomorrow."

"Jackson is here?"

"Yeah, he is waiting outside. Ryan is still at the scene and probably filling out paperwork." She saw Zach take a breath and then look deeply into her eyes. "Trent is dead, angel." Zach's voice sounded flat.

Cassie looked at Zach in shock. *Dead? How do you kill evil?*

"When Trent ran, he went down the road to the quarries. The road was wet and slippery, and he was going too fast to make the turn at the lake. Factor in the tires were practically bald and the engine was overheating, making his visibility probably zero. His car went off the drop and into the lake. I went in after him, but he was already dead."

Cassie blinked as the news sunk in.

"It's really over? Danny is dead?" She knew she shouldn't feel relief at another human being's death, but she couldn't help it. She hadn't realized that she had been holding her breath for two years until she slowly exhaled. She looked at Jillian.

"It's over, Jill. You're free, too, you know. I am so sorry you had to go through this. You're the best friend I ever had, and you shouldn't have had to go through this." Cassie felt the hot tears again as they ran down her face

"I can't think of anyone I would rather be in danger with than you, Cass. Gosh, life is going to be so boring now. How will we stand it?" Jillian smirked.

Cassie couldn't believe she was laughing and crying at the same time, but if anyone could do it to her, it was Jillian.

Zach stroked her hair as the nurse came in to give her the pain medication.

"Get some rest, Cassie. You are going to need it. Chase is going to be a pain in the ever-lovin' ass when he wakes up."

* * * *

Zach's prediction turned out to be true. After the first day at home, which Chase spent mostly sleeping, he was a real pain in the ass. Once Chase started feeling better, he chafed at having to rest.

Having to rest made him cranky, and he took that mood out on everyone around him. Cassie was so grateful that Chase was alive. The bullet had missed any vital organs but had damaged the soft tissue. It would be a while before Chase had full range of motion in that arm and shoulder. Yes, she was grateful, but she had about had it with Chase's mood. He growled at everyone around him, and she was trying desperately not to growl back.

"You have an evil look in your eyes, Cassie."

Cassie saw Zach laughing as he entered the kitchen.

"I was thinking that perhaps I could hide this pain pill in Chase's chili, and he might sleep for a little while. We could all get some rest."

Zach chuckled as he grabbed some grated cheese from the refrigerator and sprinkled it on top. "Remind me never to piss you off. Chase doesn't like how he feels when he takes the pills. So he doesn't take them and makes us miserable too. That's just Chase. He misses working with the horses, and he misses going to the construction sites with me. Let this be a lesson, Cassie. A bored Chase is a bad Chase. He used to drive Mom crazy when he was sick as a little kid."

"Speaking of your mother, when are your parents arriving?"

"Tonight, and Mom is madder than a wet hen at us for not letting her know about what happened. Let her get it all out when she gets here. She is pissed at me. It was my decision not to worry her, and I will take the heat for it. Got it?"

Zach looked completely serious.

"I mean it, Cassie. No trying to defend me or Chase. I already talked to my dads, and they can handle Mom. Promise?"

Cassie gave Zach a mock salute. "Yes, sir! I don't think I want to get in between you and your mom anyway. I want her to like me, Zach."

"She already does and the Dads, too. They love you because we love you. Mom has been bugging us to settle down for a while now. Just relax. Now my brothers are something else. Don't take anything they say seriously. They are good guys but still pretty immature. They are still in their partying stage and are constantly in trouble."

"Are you telling me to stay away from them?"

"No, just telling you that Parker and Logan are not the most responsible young men. They like pretty women, so they are going to love you." Zach gave a little leer.

Great, there would be four of them, not just two.

Chapter 18

Cassie looked really nervous, and his mom looked mad. Only his dads looked calm. *Fucking fantastic.*

"So you and Chase decided not to call your own mother when he had been shot! Shot! I cannot believe you didn't call me! You are not too old for me to tan your hide, young man!" His mother's face was an unbecoming shade of red as she shook her finger at him. Despite facing death many times in the Middle East, his mother was the most terrifying thing of all. But he was a Harper man, and he wouldn't back down.

"We didn't want to worry you, Mom. Chase was fine."

If anything her face turned a little redder, and her finger shook a little closer to his nose. *Shit. Wrong tactic.*

"*Worry me!* Holy hell! You didn't want to worry your feeble old mother, huh? Don't do me any damn favors!"

"Now, Nancy, watch your language." His father looked mildly amused at the situation. Zach admired his dad, but he wasn't helping.

His mother swung around and narrowed her eyes at her husband of thirty-five years and put her hands on her hips.

"I haven't even begun with you, Peter, so don't get me started. I hope you like sleeping on the couch because that's where you are going to be for the next month!" His mother gave his dad a deadly glare. His dad gave his mother a bland look, the only thing betraying his emotions was a faint gulp at the mention of sleeping on the couch. He saw his dads exchange a glance, and his other dad spoke up.

"Zach and Chase are grown men. If they decided to tell you what happened in their own time, then it is their business. They told me at the same time they told you, and I'm not screaming the house down, now am I?"

Oh, shit. Did Pops really say that?

His mother crossed her arms and stared at her husbands. "Peter, looks like Aaron will be joining you on the couch."

"We didn't do it on purpose, Mom. Jillian and I were taking care of Cassie and Chase and a few days passed and it didn't seem so urgent to call. They were fine, and everything was okay."

"I told him to call you, Mom." Chase had a shit-eating grin on his face.

Zach gaped at his brother. "For that whopper of a lie, I ought to shoot you again, little brother."

His mother had calmed down a little, and he could see she was trying not to laugh at the two of them.

"There will be no more shooting in this house. No more violence of any kind. And don't try to fool me, Chase, you did not. But did anyone want to call me?" She looked around the room.

Jillian stepped forward with a smirk.

"Hello, Mrs. Harper. Remember me from bingo night? I'm Jillian, Cassie's roommate. And yes, she and I both wanted to call you. Chase was a real pain to take care of, and we both thought his mother would be the only one with the patience to deal with him."

Mrs. Harper threw up her hands in defeat. "Finally! Someone with a lick of sense in this house." She turned to Cassie with a sympathetic look.

"You poor thing! Chase in pain, and if you had the patience to take care of him, you must really love him. Welcome to the family, Cassie." Zach's mom gave Cassie a brilliant smile and held out her arms for a hug.

Cassie looked at him, and he nodded. She walked nervously over to his mother, who grabbed Cassie and gave her a big hug.

"Now, let's talk grandchildren. I was thinking four or five."

Zach groaned in embarrassment. "Mom! Leave her alone!"

* * * *

Cassie let out a big yawn and slumped against the kitchen counter. It was five in the freakin' morning on Thanksgiving, and Zach and Chase were just too damn cheerful. She scowled at Zach as he whistled while pulling the turkey out of the cooler where it had been defrosting. Zach mock scowled right back at her as he scrubbed turkey off his hands in the big stainless steel sink.

"We need to get this turkey in the oven or we won't eat until tomorrow. A bird this big is going to take hours to cook."

The bird was massive. They had an equally large one that would be deep-fried later in the day. Cassie had never had a deep-fried turkey, but the boys assured her it was delicious. They swore she would be a convert by kickoff. Maybe yes, maybe no. Jillian would also be over later in the morning to lend a hand with the cooking. She was really a gourmet cook, and Cassie was looking forward to her famous garlic mashed potatoes. Right now she wanted to go back to bed and cuddle with her guys.

Her sleepy eyes took in Chase as he bustled around the kitchen slicing onions and oranges to stuff inside the bird. He was getting better every day and getting more range of motion in his arm and shoulder. She once again said a silent thank-you that both her men were okay. Chase caught her staring at him and stuck out his tongue playfully. She would just never get over how handsome they were and how lucky she was. Even crazier, if she told them that, they would just laugh and say they were the lucky ones. She pushed off the counter and groaned, heading to the sink to wash her hands.

"Okay, how can I help? The sooner we get this bird in the oven, the sooner we can go back to bed."

She saw the guys exchange a glance and knew that something was up.

"Get the roasting pan out from that cabinet, and we will get Tom here cooking and get back to bed, Your Highness." Zach gave her ass a playful pop with the dish towel. Cassie yelped and giggled and ran to Chase.

"Protect me, Chase! Your brother is trying to hurt me!"

Chase caught her around the middle with his good arm and pulled her close. Cassie breathed in his delicious smell and cuddled closer.

"Don't baby her, Chase. She needs to help, and then maybe, if she is a very good girl, we will take her back to bed for some hanky-spanky." Zach smirked at her.

"Spanky? What am I being punished for anyway?" Cassie stuck out her lower lip and pouted. "I haven't done anything."

Chase growled. "Oh really, young lady? How about coming outside to attack Trent when I told you to stay inside the house? Or how about jumping on him and trying to wrestle the gun away from him? I think my arm is healed enough to punish you today." Chase swung his arm and gave her a soft pat on the behind.

"You are going to punish me now? That was weeks ago. And I did save your life, Chase. If I hadn't jumped on Danny he would have killed you. What about you, Zach? Do you think I need to be punished, too?" Cassie glared at both the brothers, but Zach just laughed and smiled.

"This is between you and Chase. If he thinks you need to be punished, then he needs to punish you. That's why I haven't done it for him. However, after talking to him, he is willing to go easier on you since you did save his sorry ass after all."

"Go easy on me? Screw you, Chase. I saved your life." Cassie knew she had gone too far when both brothers crossed their arms over their broad chests and looked down at her speculatively. Chase turned to Zach with an evil grin.

"Did she just tell me to fuck myself, Zach? I don't like that potty mouth on her at all, you know."

"You know, Chase, I think she did tell you to screw yourself like a lightbulb. I don't like that dirty mouth, either. Perhaps we need to show Her Highness how to behave on a national holiday?"

Just that fast, they both moved around the kitchen island, and Zach threw her over his shoulder and headed straight for the bedroom, giving her ass a few swats on his way down the hall.

"Put me down, right now. I mean it!" Cassie beat her hands on Zach's muscled back. It was like punching concrete.

"Did you hear that, Chase? She means it. I guess I better put her down."

"I don't know, Zach. If you put her down, she might try and hurt us. Especially, if *she means it*," Chase said with a taunt.

"You guys are going to pay for this! Put me down right now, you assholes!" Cassie wriggled and tried to get free, but Zach held her easily.

"I really don't like that mouth on her. Perhaps we need to put something in it to keep it quiet." Zach gave her a hard smack on the ass.

"Oww! Shit, stop it!"

Smack! Smack!

"Stop cursing, Cassie, and maybe I will put you down."

Cassie beat ineffectually against Zach's back. "I wouldn't be cursing if you weren't smacking me. Please put me down, Zach. I'll be good. I promise." Cassie stopped struggling to catch her breath. She knew Zach wouldn't let her down until he was damn well ready.

"Will you be a good girl and take your punishment from Chase?"

"I don't—"

Smack!

"Stop, Cassie. Take your punishment, and then you will get a nice reward."

Reward? "What kind of a reward?"

"The kind you will like…a lot, angel. Now, are you ready to come down?"

Hmmm…she liked their rewards. "Okay, put me…oooooff!"

Cassie found herself dumped in the middle of the king-sized bed staring up at two gorgeous, sexy men who looked like they wanted to eat her up.

Oh shit, I think I am in trouble.

* * * *

Zach tugged Cassie's pajama bottoms down her legs while Chase pulled her T-shirt over her head. Zach's mouth went dry and his heart sped up as her creamy flesh was exposed to his gaze. He wondered if he would ever get used to feeling like this when he was with Cassie. With other women, the more he was with them, the more his interest waned. With Cassie, the more he was with her, the more he wanted to be with her. He loved being with her both in and out of bed. She was smart, funny, and sexy. He still couldn't believe that she felt the same about him and Chase. They wanted to build a life with her and hoped that was what she wanted, too. He leaned over her and brushed teasing kisses on her lips and down her neck, tickling the sensitive skin until she giggled, kicking her legs, and tried to push him away.

"Enough, Zach. She needs to take her punishment now and tickle fun later." Chase gave a mock scowl, but Cassie just laughed and pouted. Zach loved to hear her laugh.

"And no pouting, sweetheart. Let's get this over with. Do you know why you are being punished?"

Cassie crossed her arms and smirked. "Because you are being a real butt about this?"

Chase shook his head. "No, and that attitude is going to cost you a little extra punishment. You are being punished for disregarding your own safety. It is our job to protect and care for you, Cassie. You are not to risk your life to protect us. We are men. The kind of men who take care of their woman. If we lost you, we would have no life. You have to trust us to take care of ourselves and to take care of you. It doesn't sound very twenty-first century, but there it is."

Zach heard Chase's voice soften and saw Cassie's eyes filled with tears. Chase was the soft touch of the two of them. He would have messed this up. He still couldn't believe that Chase was determined to punish her anyway. It seemed like a trumped-up excuse.

"So, for risking your life, you will get twenty smacks on the fanny, and for your snarky remark, another five." Chase held his hand up as Cassie started to protest vehemently. Zach guessed her bottom was already a little sore from the punishment it had taken just minutes ago from his own hand. But he just loved her ass all warm and red. It was made for his hand.

"But because I appreciate you saving my life, I am knocking off twenty for good behavior. But you will take all five with good grace and not complain, deal?" Chase arched his eyebrow in question, and Zach could see Cassie swallow hard.

"Yes, Chase. Five...with good grace."

Zach nipped at her neck. "Then we are going to love the stuffing out of you."

Cassie and Chase groaned at Zach's bad Thanksgiving joke.

"Hey, the guys in my unit said that I was a real cutup," Zach protested.

"No one, at any time in your life, has thought of you as a cutup, bro. You are way too much of a hard-ass," Chase said dryly. "Now let's get this punishment over with so we can get to the pleasure."

Personally, Zach thought Cassie seemed to get a whole lot of pleasure when she was punished, but he would play along. Chase moved Cassie into position with her hands on the footboard of the bed, her gorgeous ass offered up enticingly, and her legs spread about shoulder width apart. Her pussy was already red and swollen, and Zach could clearly see her thighs glistening with arousal. His cock hardened in reaction and tented his boxers. His brother better finish up this punishment quickly, or he was going to come in his pajamas.

Chase stood to Cassie's left and swung his arm wide and then softly tapped her right cheek, barely making contact. Cassie's head whipped around in reaction to the pulled swat. Chase just smiled.

"Face forward during your punishment, sweetheart. Now, that's one."

Cassie faced forward again as Chase stroked his fingers through her soaked pussy, drawing a soft moan. Then he drew back his arm wide again and gave her a swat on the left cheek, as softly as the first. Chase was really grinning, and Zach could see now that he never had any intention of punishing Cassie. Zach had been surprised that Chase had even talked about punishing her. He normally wasn't into the dominant stuff. Chase was just too soft-hearted.

"Two."

Another swat, softer than the first two landed.

"Three."

That last two landed quickly and barely touched her bottom.

"Four. Five."

Chase helped Cassie climb onto the bed.

"You took your punishment with good grace. Now you get your reward."

Zach crawled on the bed with Cassie and Chase and positioned himself between her thighs while Chase lay on her right side, stroking her nipples and breasts. Cassie writhed in pleasure, her eyes closed and lips slightly parted as she panted and moaned. He ran his hands up the inside of her thighs, feeling her silky-soft skin and the sticky honey that dripped from her pussy. He could smell the soft musk of her arousal, and it made his dick painfully hard. He wanted release, but Cassie needed to come first. He leaned over her mound and trailed his finger up her slit and twirled circles around her clit. Cassie bucked in response, but Chase easily held her down. Cassie may have gotten out of her punishment with Chase, but she still needed a little lesson as to who was in charge in the bedroom. She would be begging him to allow her to come soon.

He touched the tip of his tongue to her pussy and ran it up and down, never touching her clit. One glance up and he saw that Chase was busy sucking and licking Cassie's nipples. Chase was a boob man, after all. Her eyes were closed tight, and her groans of pleasure stoked his desire. He had to restrain himself from ramming his cock into her pussy to the hilt and slamming into her until they both came, hard and sweaty.

* * * *

Cassie panted with pleasure as Zach's talented tongue teased and licked her sensitive flesh. Chase's mouth was sucking on her already painfully hard nipple while his fingers stroked and pulled at the other one. The flat of Zach's tongue swiped over her clit once, then twice before sliding down to her entrance where she gushed her arousal into his mouth. He lapped it up hungrily, running his tongue in circles around her hole. He pointed his tongue, and she felt him start fucking her with his tongue, pushing farther in with each stroke.

Chase started nipping at the spot on her neck that sent her into convulsions of pleasure. She felt her mind switch off as she hovered on the edge of climax. Her body hung over the precipice, waiting for the now familiar command. Her legs started shaking as Zach moved his tongue back to her clit, giving it soft licks but not enough pressure to send her over.

"Please! Please let me come!" Cassie heard the urgency in her own voice but didn't care that she was begging. Zach's fingers traveled to her slit and worked one, then two in her tight pussy. He fucked her pussy, in and out, hitting her sweet spot on each stroke.

Zach lifted his head, and Cassie whimpered at the loss of contact. "You have permission, Cassie. Come for me and Chase."

As usual, Cassie's body responded to his commanding voice. His mouth latched on to her clit and sucked softly as his teeth gave it a nip, his fingers still fucking her tight channel in and out. Her body froze as the pleasure tightened in her abdomen and cunt painfully. Her climax ripped through her like a hurricane. White light blinded her as the pleasure ran like quicksilver through her veins, making her skin ultrasensitive and tingly. Chase held her as Zach's devilish tongue continued to torture her, the shaking and trembling of her body going on for what seemed like an eternity. When she finally came down, she opened her eyes to see Chase's tender ones staring down at her.

"Damn, sweetheart, I don't think there is anything more beautiful than watching you come."

Cassie opened her mouth, but her ability to form words was still impaired. She reached up and pulled Chase down for a wet kiss instead. Chase wrapped his arms around her and rolled her on top of him. She blinked in surprise when she saw that Chase had already donned a condom.

When had that happened?

No matter, she knew what her man wanted. She positioned herself over his hard shaft, letting her fingers stroke him up and down, teasing him slightly. Chase groaned, and his hands tightened on her hips.

"Don't play around, baby, or I really will punish you next time."

Smack! Smack!

Cassie's head flew around to see Zach's smirking at her as the heat from his spanking turned from pain into the most delicious pleasure. Her pussy dripped more moisture, and she could feel it running down her thighs. Zach's spankings always made her hot as hell, and she knew she would come hard.

"Stop making threats you won't keep, Chase. Cassie, get Chase inside you now, or I will punish you this time."

Cassie pulled a face at Zach and wriggled her ass at him, knowing what his reaction would be. "Yes, sir, Zach, sir, right away!"

Smack! Smack! Smack!

"It's clear you are asking for it, angel. And I am happy to give it to you."

The light pain from the spanking amped up her arousal, and her pussy clenched, needing to be filled. She positioned herself with Chase's cock at her entrance and slowly lowered down on each hard, delicious inch. She was so wet, he slid in easily. She could feel his girth stretching her and rubbing against her sensitive spots, moving her closer to orgasm. Chase bucked up from the bed, slamming in the last few inches, bumping against her cervix, and sending a spasm of delight up her spine. She moved slowly up, his cock sliding almost out, and then he bucked again, pounding her pussy hard and sending more tingles to her clit and nipples.

She felt Zach's hand running up and down her back, and then he pressed her forward onto Chase's chest. Her ass clenched in anticipation. She knew what he had in mind and wasn't surprised to feel the cold trickle of lube running down her ass crack. She felt him run a finger around her tight hole and then a slight pressure as it breached past the tight ring of muscles. She moaned as he found those sensitive nerves and rubbed them, sending shivers down to her toes. A second finger joined the first, and she felt him scissoring his fingers, stretching her in preparation for his beautiful cock.

"Please, Zach. Please, I need it." She heard herself beg but knew that nothing she did would make Zach go any faster. He was firmly in control—of himself and her body.

A third digit was added, and the stretch and burn almost sent her over the edge. She felt so full already with Chase's cock planted firmly in her pussy and Zach's fingers stretching ass. She needed Zach inside her, fucking her now!

"Please, Zach! God! I need it now!" The desperation in her voice made it sound breathless and small. The stroking inside her stilled.

"What is it you need, Cassie? Tell me." Zach's dark voice made her tremble with anticipation.

"I need it, Zach! Please fuck me!" She tried to press back against his hand, but Chase held her firmly.

"Fuck you? My fingers are fucking you. Tell me exactly what you want, and I will give it to you. Tell me, Cassie."

Every muscle in her body cried out as she tried to move but couldn't.

"Please, Zach! Please fuck me with your cock! I need your cock in my ass! I need it!" She sounded slightly hysterical now, but she didn't care as long as Zach gave her what she needed.

She felt him withdraw from her back hole and groaned in frustration before feeling the blunt head of his cock there instead. More lubricant trickled down her crack as she felt him push forward, much larger than the fingers that had stretched her. Her body stretched to accommodate him, and the burn sent her arousal into overdrive as he insistently pressed forward into her ass.

Between Chase's cock in her pussy and Zach's cock in her ass, she felt as if she could feel every ridge and bump inside her. He grunted as he seated himself to the hilt and wrapped her hair around his hands, tugging her up gently, so she was seated on Chase but leaning back on Zach slightly. She could feel the crinkle of the hair on their thighs and smell their masculine musk.

Chase ran his hands up her stomach and began to play with her nipples, giving them sharp tweaks, knowing she liked the bite of pain with her pleasure. They slowly began to move in and out of her, driving her closer and closer to climax. Chase would pull out almost all the way, and Zach would slam all the way in, running his steel-like shaft across the sensitive nerves in her ass. Then Zach would withdraw and Chase would pump into her, running his length across her swollen clit.

Her world narrowed to just the three of them. Chase's hands on her hips moving her up and down his cock, shiny with her juices. Zach's hand in her hair, tugging on it, while the other hand wrapped around her abdomen to give him traction as he slammed into her from behind. Her body became the instrument to their pleasure as she was to theirs, and she hovered on the brink as they rode her hard and wild.

"You better be close, Chase. I can't hold back any longer." Zach's voice sounded strained.

"Right there with you, bro. Cassie first," Chase panted.

He reached and pinched her clit, and she screamed as her release ripped through her, so powerful she slammed back against Zach. The room swirled, and her sight went white, then multicolored, as pleasure so intense she thought she might faint ran through her bones like water.

She felt Zach slam into her one last time as he went rigid, then his groan of release. She was so full, she could feel his cock pulse as he spilled his seed into the condom. Chase, too, went still as he orgasmed. His pulsing sent her into a second mini-orgasm, and her toes curled with the pleasure of watching him find his release.

They lay there, covered in sweat and her honey, and struggled to catch their breath. Zach was the first to move as he withdrew gently, kissing her neck, and then disappeared into the bathroom. Chase rolled Cassie over and pulled from her body to dispose of the condom. Zach reappeared with a warm washcloth and tenderly cleaned her before tossing it in the bathroom. The men cuddled with her as her heart slowed to a more normal rate, and her language skills returned.

"Wow, this was the best Thanksgiving ever." Her voice sounded rough even to her own ears.

She could feel their chuckles against her neck and ear.

"Best I ever had. How about you, bro?" Zach said as he propped his head on his elbow.

"Can't think of a better one, either, unless you count that Thanksgiving Uncle Dwight set fire to the garage when he was frying the turkey." Chase's voice was teasing.

"That was funny, but certainly not as pleasurable." Zach rolled over on his back and laughed at the memory.

Cassie elbowed Chase in the ribs. "A garage fire was better than this? Kind of insulting, Chase."

"No way, baby. This was much better, but that was a memorable Thanksgiving. We ate grilled cheese sandwiches that year after the fire department left. Mom was pissed, as only Mom can be. The dads spent the whole day calming her down, Jackson decided to become a firefighter, and we never let Dwight cook again."

They all stared at each other as his words sunk in and reminded them. *The turkey.*

"Shit, we need to get the turkey in the oven." Chase groaned as he sat up and swung his legs off the bed, ripping the covers away from all of them as he stood up.

"Hey!" Cassie scrambled to grab the sheet.

"Nope, if I get up to cook, everyone gets up to cook. So get your asses out of bed."

* * * *

Cassie had never eaten so much in her life. Zach and Chase were right—deep-fried turkey was great. And so was the green bean casserole, garlic mashed potatoes, gravy, stuffing, rolls, and the two slices of chocolate cake. She groaned softly and nuzzled Chase a little more closely. This was the best Thanksgiving ever. She really felt like she was part of a family. She already loved their mom, both of their dads, and their two younger brothers. Parker and Logan were charming and devastatingly handsome. Girls must be fighting to get their attention and did those boys know it, too. They were sweet but definitely aware of their effect on the opposite sex.

Jillian was relaxing with her brother, Mark and his husband, Travis. They had arrived the day before and said they were already in love with Plenty. She also noticed that Mark and Travis enjoyed flirting with Becca and making her blush. Becca was enjoying a piece of pie with her dad and Dr. Steve. The only ones missing were Ryan and Jackson. Both were on duty but were due any minute.

A noise at the door caught her attention, and she saw Zach heading to greet Ryan and Jackson and pushing them back out the front door. Cassie nudged a dozing Chase.

"Hey, Ryan and Jackson are here. I need to fix them some food so let me up, handsome."

Chase jumped awake with a start. "I'll do it, sweetheart. You rest here." He pressed her back on the cushions.

Cassie frowned at Chase. "I can help, Chase. You need to rest. I think you overdid it this morning," said Cassie with a smirk.

"It was my pleasure, babe. Now stay put."

Cassie watched Chase walk toward the kitchen. Yep, something was definitely going on. Chase and Zach had been jumpy all day and had been exchanging glances constantly. What were her boys up to?

Zach and Chase walked in a moment later.

"Can we have everyone's attention, please?" Zach stood in front of the fireplace as everyone stopped talking and turned to him.

"Thank you. First of all, we want to thank everyone for sharing this Thanksgiving with us. It is our first with Cassie but hopefully just the first of many more. Cassie came into our lives just three months ago, but Chase and I haven't been the same since the day we met her. We love her, and her friends are now our friends." An "awww" went up from the group.

"Cassie has been through a lot these last few years, so Chase and I wanted to give her something special to show her how thankful we are that we found her. Chase?"

Cassie turned to see Chase walking toward her with something in his arms. At first, she didn't know what it was, but as he got closer her eyes filled with tears. *They remembered!*

Chase handed the soft, squirmy, and very furry puppy to her. Tears flowed freely as she cuddled the puppy to her face. He squirmed and began to lick her tears and tried to climb onto her shoulder.

"It's a Golden Retriever puppy, Cassie. Jillian said they were your favorite." Zach and Chase both knelt next to her as she petted and kissed the dog. She ran her hands over the soft fur and saw that it was wearing the cutest red collar with a little tag. Had they already named him?

Cassie lifted the tag to read it and sobbed even harder when she read the words "Will you marry us?"

Cassie looked up to see both Zach and Chase on their knees in front of her.

"Will you marry us, angel? We can't imagine life without you." Zach leaned in and softly kissed her lips nervously.

"We know it's fast, but Zach and I love you more than anything. Will you marry us?"

Cassie couldn't believe they were nervous. They had just given her an engagement dog, after all.

"Yes! Yes! Yes! Of course I will marry you both." Cassie launched herself at them, hugging them so tightly the puppy wriggled free to sniff his new home.

"Thank goodness. We thought you might turn us down," Zach said with a laugh. He then pulled a box from behind him and opened it up to reveal an emerald cut diamond ring nestled between two trillions.

"Oh my god, there's a ring, too?" Cassie thought she might faint. A dog, a marriage proposal, and a ring? She must be dreaming.

Zach and Chase each helped her slip the ring on her finger.

Zach and Chase's mother smiled. "Looks like champagne is in order. I got myself a daughter. *Finally!*"

The whole crowd laughed and joked as they offered their congratulations. It felt so right being there with Zach and Chase and their family and friends. She was going to get a lifetime of this happiness.

"What are you thinking, Cassie?" Cassie smiled up at Zach and Chase.

"I was just thinking that Jillian and Becca should be this happy, too." She looked at how Ryan and Jackson stared at Jillian like she was a goddess and how Mark and Travis kept trying to get close to Becca.

"I think they will be, too, boys. It is only a matter of time."

Cassie scooped up the puppy and gave him a big kiss. "Right, Duffy?"

Duffy licked her face in agreement.

THE END

LARAVALENTINE.NET
LARAVALENTINEAUTHOR@GMAIL.COM

ABOUT THE AUTHOR

I've been a dreamer my entire life. So, it was only natural to start writing down some of those stories that I have been dreaming about.

Being the hopeless romantic that I am, I fall in love with all of my characters. They are perfectly imperfect with the hopes, dreams, desires, and flaws that we all have. I want them to overcome obstacles and fear to get to their happily ever after. We all should. Everyone deserves their very own sexy, happily ever after.

I grew up in the cold, but beautiful plains of Illinois. I now live in Central Florida with my handsome husband—who's a real, native Floridian—and my son whom I have dubbed "Louis the Sun King." They claim to be supportive of all the time I spend on my laptop, but they may simply be resigned to my need to write.

When I am not working at my conservative day job or writing furiously, I enjoy relaxing with my family or curling up with a good book.

Also by Lara Valentine

Everlasting Classic: The Martinis and Chocolate Book Club 1: *Doctor's Orders*
Ménage Everlasting: Plenty, FL 2: *Plenty to Learn*

Available at
BOOKSTRAND.COM

Siren Publishing, Inc.
www.SirenPublishing.com